"Miss, are you all right?"

Danny bent to pick up the puppy and looked the little girl in the eyes. "I want you to know that Holly has a fine warm house now and plenty to eat. She's going to be very happy, and you may come and visit her whenever you wish."

"Truly?" Jane's niece wiped her eyes on her sleeve and patted the puppy's head.

"For sure and certain," Danny said.

"Okay. Goodbye, Holly. Don't forget me."

Danny tipped his hat toward Jane and spoke softly, "*Danki* for my early Christmas gift."

"*Du bischt wilkumm.*"

He straightened in surprise. "You speak Deitch?"

"I have to go. There's work to do." Jane spun around and hurried toward the house, giving her uncle a sidelong glance while keeping well away from him. Danny grew sick to his stomach. This woman and child had been abused; he was sure of it.

And there was nothing he could do…

After thirty-five years as a nurse, **Patricia Davids** hung up her stethoscope to become a full-time writer. She enjoys spending her free time visiting her grandchildren, doing some long-overdue yard work and traveling to research her story locations. She resides in Wichita, Kansas. Pat always enjoys hearing from her readers. You can visit her online at patriciadavids.com.

Books by Patricia Davids

Love Inspired

North Country Amish

An Amish Wife for Christmas
Shelter from the Storm
The Amish Teacher's Dilemma
A Haven for Christmas
Someone to Trust
An Amish Mother for His Twins
Mistaken for His Amish Bride
Christmas on His Doorstep

The Amish Bachelors

An Amish Harvest
An Amish Noel
His Amish Teacher
Their Pretend Amish Courtship
An Unexpected Amish Romance
His New Amish Family

Visit the Author Profile page at LoveInspired.com for more titles.

Christmas on His Doorstep

Patricia Davids

LOVE INSPIRED
INSPIRATIONAL ROMANCE

LOVE INSPIRED®
INSPIRATIONAL ROMANCE

Recycling programs
for this product may
not exist in your area.

ISBN-13: 978-1-335-58614-8

Christmas on His Doorstep

For questions and comments about the quality of this book, please contact us
at CustomerService@Harlequin.com.

Love Inspired
22 Adelaide St. West, 41st Floor
Toronto, Ontario M5H 4E3, Canada
www.LoveInspired.com

Printed in U.S.A.

And they brought young children to him,
that he should touch them: and his disciples
rebuked those that brought them.

But when Jesus saw it, he was much displeased,
and said unto them, Suffer the little children
to come unto me, and forbid them not:
for of such is the kingdom of God.
—*Mark* 10:13–14

This book is dedicated to my constant companion,
my mood booster, my jester, my sounding board
and my giver of endless, unconditional love.
Dear Sugar, without your wildly wagging tail,
excited yipping and laugh-out-loud antics,
my life would be boring beyond words.

Chapter One

❧

"I don't want to leave Holly here, Auntie Jane. She's scared."

Tears filled her eyes, but Jane Christner ignored her five-year-old niece's pleading and tied the puppy's rope to the doorknob of a house at the edge of town in New Covenant. She didn't want to abandon Holly either, but what choice did she have?

"The man who lives here is the teacher we saw playing with that big yellow dog, remember? He'll find a wonderful home for Holly."

The poor animal deserved someone to care for her the way Jane wanted to but couldn't. Bridget loved the puppy, but love alone couldn't provide the food the little dog desperately needed.

Bridget sniffed as she stroked Holly's head. The pup knew something was wrong. She pressed close to Bridget and gazed at Jane with worried eyes.

Bridget glanced at Jane. "Are you sure he's nice?"

"I am."

It had been the sound of children's laughter that drew Jane to the edge of the woods near the school last week. Ordinarily, she never went close to the village while foraging for wild edibles. Worried about the puppy Bridget had found by the side of the road and their own lack of food, Jane ventured closer to the village than she intended. When she heard the children's shouts of joy, she wanted to see what was making them so happy.

What she saw were Amish schoolchildren out for recess. The sight instantly transported her back to her youth. Fun. Security. That's what she remembered about growing up in an Amish community.

Before God took it all away from her.

That day she caught sight of an Amish man pushing a red-haired, freckled-faced little girl on a swing.

"Higher, teacher," the child shouted.

A man for a teacher? That surprised Jane. Only female schoolteachers had taught in her community.

As she had watched, a big yellow hound bounded up to the teacher with a ball in her mouth. He'd ruffled the dog's ears, thrown the ball and gone back to swinging the child until the dog returned. Laughing, he threw the ball again. The sound of his easy, affectionate laugher touched something deep inside Jane. She knew he was a good man.

"They're having fun," Bridget had whispered in awe.

The dog dashed away with the ball to where the children were getting up a game of softball, then ran to the outfield and waited for the ball to come her way. When it did, she snatched it up before racing after the runner until a laughing student caught her and took back the ball. Everyone praised the dog, including the teacher, who pulled out his kerchief, dried the ball before giving it back to the pitcher.

"But why can't Holly stay with us?" Bridget's tearful voice jerked Jane back to the present.

"We can't take care of her, sweetie."

Bridget wiped her nose on the back of her sleeve. "'Cause Uncle Albert doesn't like her."

It was true. "Albert doesn't want to feed her anymore. You don't want her to be hungry. This man will take care of her."

Albert Newcomb had no use for things that couldn't earn their keep. Things like a stray puppy or his niece, Jane. His great-niece Bridget, however, brought in a monthly stipend from the state. Free money, he claimed. Funds he seldom spent on the child's care.

The stipend had arrived today. Albert would be in town stocking up on liquor and, hopefully, food, if he was in a generous mood. Jane had seized the chance while he was out to bring the puppy here.

"Uncle is mean," Bridget whispered.

"Never let him hear you say that." His temper needed little provocation to explode.

Jane glanced at her niece's gaunt face. Bridget looked so much like her mother, with her sleek red hair, freckles and green eyes, only Lois's cheeks had been plump and rosy. Guilt stabbed Jane's heart at the way she'd failed her sister.

I'm doing the best I can for your daughter, Lois, but I know it's not enough. Forgive me. I love her like she's my child, Lois. Sometimes I forget she isn't.

Lois had been gone four years already. Four hard years. Life wasn't fair. Why did a merciful God allow it?

Bitterness pushed aside Jane's guilt. God took her parents, then her only sister, leaving her and Bridget to suffer at the hands of Albert's drunken rages. Her faith had died a long time ago. Trapped with no job, nowhere to go in an isolated part of northern Maine, Jane did what she could to eke out an existence and protect Bridget.

At least she could give this little dog a chance at a better life.

Biting cold made her fingers fumble with the rope. Fat snowflakes drifted down.

"Holly can have some of my food." Bridget's eyes glistened with unshed tears.

There was never enough food because Albert withheld it to punish Jane. Bridget had missed too many meals because of his claims the child was clumsy or stupid.

Jane focused on tying the rope, repressing her anger. Bridget wouldn't go to bed hungry tonight if she hurried. Jane had seen a large wild rosebush loaded with rose hips close to the school. She'd gather some on the way back to make a filling rose hip soup.

The puppy whined, a pitiful sound that tore at Jane's heart. The Amish schoolteacher seemed like a good man. Jane hoped a child from the school would adopt the sweet little dog and love her.

Finally, Jane secured the knot. Tucking a note of explanation under the rope around the puppy's neck, she stroked the English setter's soft, white speckled head one last time. "You be good for this fellow, Holly."

School would let out soon. Jane didn't want

to be seen in the village. Albert would be furious if he found out. He'd forbidden them to have any contact with the Amish.

The door in front of her opened unexpectedly. The man she'd seen with the children looked down. Astonishment filled his dark brown eyes. "Hello. Can I help you?"

Jane's heart jumped to her throat. Why was he here? He should be in the school. She stumbled backward. Now that he'd seen her, Albert might find out where she'd gone. She grabbed Bridget's hand and ran toward the woods as fast as she could.

"Hey, wait!" Danny Coblentz stared at the fleeing pair. What was going on? He glanced down and saw a rope tied to his doorknob. At the other end, a scrawny puppy crept toward his feet.

"Wait! What about your dog?" The fleeing pair didn't stop.

He tried to follow, but the puppy tangled the rope around his feet.

Was this some kind of joke?

By the time he freed himself, the woman and child had vanished into the woods. His brother-in-law Willis Gingrich came around from behind the school. "Were you hollering for me, Danny?"

"*Nee*, I wanted to stop that woman."

Willis gazed toward the woods. "Why was she running?"

"I don't know." He'd had only a brief glimpse of the pair, but he didn't know them.

Willis looked at the puppy. "When did you get a dog?"

Danny pointed toward the trees. "That woman tied this puppy to my door and ran off."

"That's odd. The poor thing looks like it's starving." Willis kneeled to stroke the pup. "She's not very old. Three or four months at most. Hey, there's a note under the collar."

Willis handed it to Danny. "My reading is improving, but I'm slow."

Willis, along with his younger brother Otto, suffered from dyslexia. Ashamed of his inability to read, Willis had hidden the fact until Danny's sister Eva, who had been the teacher in New Covenant before Danny, discovered Willis's secret and showed him it was nothing to be ashamed of. The two fell in love and married two years ago.

Danny scanned the note then read it aloud. "'This is Holly. Please find her a home.'"

"That's all it says?"

Danny kneeled beside the dog. "Hello, Holly. Did they name you that because of your red speckles? Who is the woman who left you? Why leave you with me?" She licked his hand.

"Maybe they heard you're a soft touch." Willis chuckled. "What are you going to do with her?"

Danny looked up hopefully. "Would you like a dog?"

"Nee."

"I guess I'll take her inside, then try to locate the mystery woman. She wore *Englisch* clothing. The child had on pink boots. Her face was thin, Willis. Much too thin for a healthy child." The woman's face had been gaunt, too. Her large dark eyes full of fear.

"Do you think the child is sick?"

"Maybe malnourished."

"Perhaps they gave up the dog because they don't have enough to eat themselves."

"That's possible." Danny's determination to discover the truth grew.

As a teacher, he kept a close eye on all the *kinder* under his care. No child in his community would go hungry if he could help it, even if she wasn't his student. Or Amish.

The puppy whined pitifully. First things first. Holly needed his attention. The late November cold made it impossible to leave her outside.

The school doors opened across the way. The children poured out. Maddie, a fourth-grade student, waved at Willis, racing for home behind her fourteen-year-old brother Otto. They were Willis's half-siblings. Along with seventeen-year-old Harley who worked with Willis in his blacksmith shop, the children came to live with him when they were orphaned a few years ago.

Willis jerked his thumb toward his house across the road. "I'd better get home. I left Harley in charge of baby Ruth. Do you have dog food?"

Danny shook his head. "*Nee,* but I'll find something."

"Don't feed her too much. Might make her sick."

"*Danki.* Tell Eva I appreciate her covering for me this afternoon."

"Your sister loves to substitute teach, so ask her anytime. Between you and me, I think she was glad to get out of the house for a couple of hours. Ruth is a *goot bobbli,* but Eva needed the break."

After Willis left, Danny picked up the pup. She tried to lick his face. He pulled away. "No kisses. Let's get you in out of the cold. Then I'm going to find your mistress. She has some explaining to do."

He found an old towel, lined a cardboard box with it, set it near the stove in his kitchen and placed the pup inside. She stood with her paws on the rim whining.

"Nope, you've got to stay in there for now."

Opening the refrigerator, he stared at the contents. What would the dog like that would be good for her? Leftovers were sparse because he took most of his meals with Eva and her family. At the back, he located a plate with leftover baked chicken that Eva had sent home with him two days before. After shredding it, he added some canned peas and carrots. Mashing it all together, he warmed it on the stove, then put a cupful in a bowl.

He lifted Holly from the box and put her down beside the food. She snarfed it up so quickly he considered giving her more but decided against it. Licking her chops, she gazed at him hopefully. Poor little thing.

"Sorry. That's all for now, but there will be more later."

He took a knife and cut away one side of the box so she could get in and out easily. After making sure she had water within reach, he shut her in the kitchen, put on his overcoat and went outside.

It was snowing heavily now. He found the path the pair had taken into the forest. The Zook children regularly used it when they walked to school. The path ended at a narrow dirt road leading farther back into the woods. He passed the Zook farm but several hundred yards farther on, he had to admit defeat. Whatever footprints might have remained were quickly being covered with fresh snow.

He walked back and saw Jedidiah Zook coming out of the barn. He hailed the farmer. "Jed, have you got a minute?"

"Sure. What brings you out this way?" Jed frowned suddenly. "Have my *kinder* been misbehaving at school?"

In the past year, Jed had gained two daughters when his orphaned nieces Polly and Lydia arrived to stay with him. Then he'd gained a stepson last fall when he married the boy's widowed mother. Parenting was new to him.

"Nothing like that," Danny assured him. "Matthew is shy, but he and the girls are *goot* scholars. This is going to sound strange, but a woman with a little girl left a puppy at my place. They came this way about twenty minutes ago. Did you see them or know who they are? They're not Amish. The woman looked to be in her early twenties. Dark hair, dark eyes. The girl is four or five with red hair. She had on pink boots."

"Doesn't sound like anyone I know. Let's ask the missus." He nodded toward the house.

Mary Beth Zook couldn't help. "We're the

last Amish farm in this direction. There are a couple of *Englisch* farms on the other side of the creek, but I don't know any of those folks. I'm sorry, Danny."

He swallowed his disappointment. "*Danki,* anyway."

"Polly and Lydia are getting excited about their Christmas program. I'm eager to see it myself." She smiled at her husband. "It will be our first Christmas together as a family."

"I'll try to make it memorable." Danny tamped down a twinge of envy. Mary Beth and Jedidiah were clearly in love. Something Danny hadn't been able to find. The Lord had seen fit to fashion a happy family out of their heartaches, but Danny wondered if his turn to find love would ever come.

When he entered his kitchen a short time later, the puppy greeted him like a long-lost friend but went to the door as if expecting someone else. She whined, scratching at the wood.

Danny ruffled her silky ears. "It's only me. Tomorrow is Saturday. We'll go farther into the woods together. Maybe you can show me the way home."

Jane ran until her burning lungs and a painful stitch in her side forced her to stop. She lowered Bridget to the ground and leaned against a tree trunk until she caught her breath. The heavy snow made it difficult going.

"Is that bad man chasing us?" Bridget asked fearfully.

Jane shook her head. "He's not a bad man. I'm in a hurry to get home and finish the chores before Uncle gets back from town. You know how upset he gets if things aren't to his liking."

Jane thought regretfully about the rose hips she hadn't been able to gather.

"I'll help you do the chores. I like Mable. She's a nice milk cow, but she isn't a dog."

Pressing a hand to her aching side, Jane managed a smile. "She isn't, but she gives us milk and cream."

"Can I milk her tonight?"

Mable could get restless in the stanchion. The thought of her stepping on Bridget's small foot made Jane shake her head. "Not until you are a little older."

"Auntie Jane, can we live somewhere else? If we didn't stay with Uncle Albert, we could keep Holly."

If only Bridget realized how desperately Jane wanted to do exactly that.

Albert was Bridget's legal guardian. As their only living relative, he had been Jane's guardian, too, until she turned eighteen. Albert told her to leave then, but he refused to let Bridget go with her. Jane stayed on, working herself to the bone trying to keep a roof over their heads and eke out a living from the farm while Albert did nothing but stare at his TV or take the occasional odd job in town. As hard as it was to live under his thumb, leaving without Bridget was impossible. Jane had to protect her.

"Someday we'll have a place of our own." Jane hoped they weren't empty words. Even if she convinced Albert to relinquish custody of Bridget, she had no job, no place of her own and no money. All things she needed to be considered a suitable guardian.

"Let's get home, Brie." She took Bridget's hand and started walking. At least she'd given the puppy a hopefully better life.

By the time Albert returned from town that evening Jane had finished feeding the pigs, chickens and the cow, fixed the pig's fence again, shoveled the snow from in front of the run-down cabin and raked it off the porch roof to keep it from collapsing.

When Albert got out of his car, he looked around. "Did you get rid of that mutt like I told you?"

"I did." She kept her eyes down. He hadn't meant for her to give the puppy away when he told her to get rid of it once and for all.

"Good. You should have shoveled a path to the barn."

"I was about to get started on that."

"Do it later. I've got some groceries you need to put away. I thought you could fix a meatloaf. It's the one meal you make that isn't half bad. That kid's money doesn't go as far as it used to. I don't know how the state expects me to take care of her on a pittance."

Jane was too excited to hear he had brought food home to be bothered by his complaints. "I'll get supper started right away."

She carried the bags of food inside and opened the refrigerator. The cabin had electricity, but Albert allowed only the fridge, two lamps, the phone with an answering machine and his TV in the house. He refused to have electric heaters burning up his money. Wood was free but hard work for Jane to gather enough to last the winter. In the barn, there was a single lightbulb along with an electric tank heater to keep the water for the animals from freezing. Jane used it sparingly, chopping through the ice with an ax when it wasn't too thick. Up in the house's loft where Bridget and Jane shared a bed, there was only a bare bulb hanging from the ceiling for light.

After putting the meatloaf in to bake, she climbed to the loft where Bridget sat under the covers on the bed with her tattered picture book tilted toward the light. The child sniffled quietly. Seeing her sadness twisted Jane's heart. Bridget didn't have Holly, but at least she wouldn't go to bed hungry tonight. "Guess what we're having for supper, Bridget?"

Bridget didn't look up. "What?"

"Meatloaf." Jane would make sure she saved back an extra slice for Bridget before she put the dish on the table. What Albert didn't know wouldn't hurt him.

"Yum!" Bridget held the book out to Jane. "Will you read me a story from Momma's book?"

Jane clasped the sketchbook to her chest as she slipped into bed with the child. It was Bridget's most treasured possession. The only thing she owned that had belonged to her mother. Jane had made sure Bridget knew Lois had drawn each picture for her baby. Jane used it to keep Bridget's connection to her mother alive. The sketchbook contained dozens of wonderful drawings of Lois's time in the city, but it didn't have stories. Those Jane made up to go along with the pictures.

"Which story do you want? 'The Christmas Gift'? I know it's your favorite."

"Is there one about a dog?"

Jane leafed through the sketches until she came to the one of a woman walking a poodle in the park. She closed her eyes a moment to form the start of the story. "This is about Missy Muffin."

Bridget giggled. "That's a funny name for a dog."

"Oh, that isn't the dog's name. That's the name of the woman who owns Motley Mutt. Once upon a time, Missy Muffin and Motley Mutt went for a walk in the city."

"Wait." Bridget's lower lip quivered. "Do they live happily ever after?"

Sorrow squeezed Jane's heart. "Yes, they have wonderful adventures together."

"Do you think I'll ever see Holly again?"

It was doubtful, but Jane couldn't bear to take all hope away from the child who had lost so much already. "Maybe."

"I'm going to ask God to let her visit me when I say my prayers tonight."

Jane had taught Bridget to pray but she had given up asking God for favors a long time ago. She kissed the top of Bridget's head. "You do that."

Maybe He would listen to an innocent child.

Chapter Two

❧

"Are you leading me on a wild-goose chase through the Maine woods?"

Holly didn't answer Danny, but they had tramped for nearly three miles already. He'd stopped at several *Englisch* farms near the road that led back into the forest, but none of the people recognized the puppy. At the last farm where he'd stopped, Danny learned only one cabin remained farther on, but the man who owned it didn't like visitors. The farmer Danny spoke with said he'd seen a woman and child a few times but had never talked to them.

Danny shifted the satchel with his supplies more comfortably on his shoulder. Only a greenhorn or a fool ventured into the woods unprepared. He had two bottles of water, a fire starter kit, a half pound of moose jerky that he could share with the dog and a blanket. He could carry the puppy in it if he needed. She would be tired long before they got home.

Holly turned off the roadway and led him into a clearing. A ramshackle cabin stood beyond a fenced garden. The woman who had tied Holly to his doorknob stood by a woodpile with an ax in her hand.

"Sorry I doubted you, girl. This is the place."

Holly jumped, tugging at the rope, barking excitedly. The woman began frantically waving Danny back. Glancing around to see if he had stumbled into something he shouldn't have, he saw only a snow-covered field. Not about to go away before he had some answers, he walked toward her.

The farm didn't appear prosperous. Equipment used to plant and harvest potatoes sat beside a leaning barn, but they were rusty hulks. Three cars and two pickups in various stages of deterioration sat in amongst the snow-covered weeds with their hoods raised. A thin cow and a half-dozen young pigs occupied a corral with a haphazard fence that looked like it would come down in a strong wind. The windows of the cabin had plastic sheeting nailed over them. The porch dipped heavily on one end.

The woman rushed toward him, stopping a few feet away. "Go. Take the dog and go away."

The fear in her voice and eyes shocked him.

Trying to look friendly, he smiled. "It's nice to see you again. I'm Danny Coblentz. I'll go, but only after I hear why you abandoned this pup on my porch."

"What is he doing here?" A portly older man with a scraggly gray beard and a fierce frown shouted from the sagging front porch.

The woman took a step closer to Danny. She clasped her hands together. "Please, I'm begging you. Take Holly and go away."

An old bruise on her delicate jaw looked suspiciously like a handprint. Her dark eyes pleaded with him to do as she asked, but he hesitated. Something wasn't right here.

"Get off my land. You're trespassing," the man shouted. He picked up the stout piece of firewood from the stack by the door and advanced toward Danny.

"I mean no harm." Danny kept his friendliest smile in place. "I'm out for a walk with my new dog. She led me here."

"I told you to get rid of that mutt, Jane. Do I have to do everything myself?" He smacked the piece of firewood into his palm. The puppy dropped to her belly beside Danny.

Jane spun around, stepping between Danny and the advancing, irate man. "I'm sorry, Uncle Albert. I thought finding her a new home would make it easier on Bridget. You know how much she likes the little dog."

"You gave her to one of those holier-than-thou hypocrites?"

"Holly! You brought her home!" The child came flying out of the house toward Danny and the dog. She hadn't bothered to put a coat over her plain blue dress. Holly lunged and barked eagerly, trying to reach the child.

Albert turned around and raised his hand. "Get back in the house."

Bridget darted around him and fell to her knees at Danny's side, hugging the puppy as the excited dog covered her face with kisses.

"Don't disobey me," Albert snarled.

Jane snatched up Bridget, who started crying. "You need to go, sir. Don't come back."

Every fiber of his being said to stay. These weren't his students or even Amish folks, but they were in trouble. They were both too thin. Albert, on the other hand, didn't look as if he had missed any meals. Bridget's threadbare too-small dress had been neatly patched and lengthened with a strip of another fabric. She had on her pink boots, but the heel of one had duct tape covering it. There was nothing shameful about being poor, but he sensed it was more than that.

"Please go," Jane whispered.

What had he stumbled into? "Miss, are you okay?"

"I'm fine," she said too quickly.

Danny picked up the dog and looked Bridget in the eyes. "Holly has a warm house now and plenty to eat. You may come visit her whenever you wish."

"Truly?" Bridget wiped her eyes on her sleeve.

"For sure and certain," Danny said.

"Okay. Goodbye, Holly. Don't forget me."

Danny straightened and looked at Albert. "Sorry for disrupting your morning. I'll be on my way now."

"And don't come back. You Amish are always sneaking around looking to trick a man out of his possessions." His palpable rage worried Danny.

He tipped his hat toward Jane. "*Danki* for my early Christmas gift."

"Du bischt wilkumm."

"You speak Deitsh?" That surprised him.

"I must go. There's work to do." She spun around and hurried toward the house, giving her uncle a sidelong glance while keeping well away from him. Danny's stomach roiled as helplessness filled him. This woman and child were victims of abuse, and he could do nothing about it.

Albert looked Danny up and down. "I should make you pay for that pup."

Danny didn't bother replying. He would have gladly given Jane money for the dog, but he suspected she wouldn't see a cent if he gave it to Albert.

He carried the puppy out of the clearing and put her on the ground when he was well away. She glanced back, whining repeatedly but stayed beside him.

"Don't worry. I'll do something. I just don't know what yet." Danny couldn't walk away and forget about Holly's family any more than the puppy could.

He gazed back at the farmstead through the trees. If only he could speak to Jane alone.

Jane set Bridget on the floor inside the cabin. "Go up to our loft and sweep the floor. Don't come down until I call you."

"He's mad. I'm scared for you."

"It'll be okay. Think about how happy Holly is to have a warm house, food and a kind owner. We did the right thing."

"I guess. He seems nice."

Danny Coblentz was everything Jane remembered from seeing him with the schoolchildren. Except maybe better looking up close with kind brown eyes and a friendly smile. She had noticed that much about him during their brief meeting. No beard meant he wasn't a married

Amish fellow. His comforting words to Bridget warmed Jane's heart. She'd chosen wisely when she left the puppy with him.

Confusion and concern had been written plainly on his face when Albert threatened him. Danny Coblentz wanted to aid them. She saw that, but he couldn't help. Taking care of Holly was enough. It was a relief to know the puppy had a better life ahead of her.

"Why doesn't Uncle like Amish people?" Bridget asked.

"I don't know. Something happened a long time ago that made him distrust Amish folks, but the Amish people I remember growing up were gentle and caring."

Albert, her mother's brother, had lived in the same community where Jane grew up. His sister left their Mennonite faith and joined the Amish church to marry the man she loved. Shortly before the accident that took Jane's parents, Albert moved away. Jane never knew why. After the accident, Jane went to stay with her only sister in Utica.

Jane thought it would be a temporary arrangement. She expected her sister to return to the family farm, but Lois refused and sold the property. Jane was left to hope her bishop could find someone in their Amish community to take her in permanently. The Amish looked after one another. But then she learned her unwed sister was pregnant. She stayed to help take care of Lois and the baby.

The outside door slammed open, jerking Jane back to the present. Bridget scurried up the ladder to the loft. Jane added a log to the fireplace.

"I can't believe you gave that mutt to an Amishman. What were you thinking?"

Jane swallowed hard and tried for a disinterested tone. "Her whining annoyed you to no end. I thought it would amuse you to know I left her with an Amish fellow."

"I hope she keeps him up all night the way she did me. I don't want to find him sneaking around here again. You got that?"

"Why would he come back?" Why did she wish he would?

"I saw you making eyes at him." There was a meanness in his voice she dreaded.

She moved to clear the breakfast dishes from the table. "You're mistaken."

He grabbed her upper arm, jerking her around to face him. "I saw what I saw. You can go anytime, with anyone you fancy, but Bridget stays with me. I'm her legal guardian. You take her without my permission and that's kidnapping. You'll go to jail for a long, long time and she'll still be with me."

A sliver of defiance came from out of nowhere. Jane lifted her chin. "Without me you'd have to tend the farm, chop your own firewood and do your own cooking. Have you thought of that?"

"I'd manage," he scoffed.

Jane saw a flicker of uncertainty in his eyes. It bolstered her courage. "Not for long, I'm thinking."

His expression hardened. "Bridget's old enough to do the chores and handle an ax."

"She's five."

He turned away. "When she gets cold enough, she'll learn what she needs to do. Bridget! Get down here and go feed the pigs!"

Bridget came down the ladder and stood by Jane, looking uncertain. "I don't know how."

He leaned toward her. "Sure you do. You fill a five-gallon bucket with mash, mix it with some of the milk from the cow and dump it in their trough. You can manage the milking, right? You've watched your aunt enough. Be careful you don't get in the pen with the pigs though. Hungry hogs will take a bite out of you quick as a wink." He snapped his teeth together.

Bridget hid her face against Jane's leg.

"Never mind, Bridget. I'll feed them." Jane's defiance leaked away. Albert had beaten her. He knew it.

A self-satisfied chuckle burst from him. "Your auntie watches out for you, Bridget."

Bridget took hold of Jane's hand. "I know."

Albert nodded toward the front door. "Bring in a load of firewood while your aunt does her chores. Did Jane tell you she's thinking about leaving us?"

Laughing, he crossed the room, sat in his chair by the fireplace and stared at the flickering screen of a small television.

Bridget's stricken expression tore at Jane's heart. Dropping to her knees, Jane embraced the trembling child. Bridget locked her arms around Jane's neck. "You're not going to leave me, are you Auntie Jane?"

"*Nee.* Of course not. I'll never leave you, *liebchen.* Never. I promise."

"I believe you. He's being mean again," Bridget whispered.

"And we don't believe the things he says when he's mean, do we?" Jane whispered back.

"No. I'm not stupid. Neither are you. We're not worthless or clumsy or good for nothing."

"That's right. I love you and you love me. We're strong together. Now, you'd better go bring in some wood. Don't try to take too much at once and put on your coat."

Jane lifted the milk pail from beside the sink.

She could hear her uncle chuckling as she walked out the door.

On the porch, Jane gazed toward the place where Danny Coblentz had disappeared. There were still good men in the world. She forgot that sometimes. The memory of his kindness to Bridget would stay with her as a reminder in the years ahead.

Once Bridget turned eighteen, Albert would have no right to keep her. Without her care funds from the state, he'd likely be glad to see her go. Thirteen more years and they would be free. It stretched like an eternity before Jane. What her baby girl would have to endure until then brought tears to Jane's eyes.

Her only chance to change their future before that hinged on Bridget starting school next year. With Bridget safely away from Albert during the day, Jane could get a job and save enough money to get her own place. She would need to prove to the court that she could offer a better living situation.

Albert might insist Bridget be homeschooled. That would put a kink in Jane's plan, but if he didn't, within a year, she could apply to become Bridget's guardian. Albert would fight it. So far, he had won every battle.

With flagging spirits, she crossed the farm-yard, entered the barn and paused, waiting for her eyes to adjust to the dim light. A puppy whined.

"Don't be scared," Danny said softly.

Jane blew out a deep breath. "I'm not, but you shouldn't be here."

She wasn't screaming or running away. The two things that Danny thought were most likely to happen. In fact, she appeared surprisingly calm. She tilted her head slightly. "How did you know I would be the one who came to do chores?"

"The cow has a full udder, so I knew she hadn't been milked yet. You were dressed in boots and a heavy coat. Your uncle had on house slippers. I made an educated guess."

"And if you had guessed wrong?"

"I've been watching the house through that window. If I'd seen your uncle coming this way, I would've slipped out the back door into the woods."

"Aren't you worried that he'll come out to help me?"

Danny eyed her closely. "You don't look worried. I'm going to assume he doesn't do the milking."

She opened the side door and let the milk cow in. Danny took off his satchel, laid it aside, then grabbed a pitchfork to throw hay into the feed bunk. The cow put her head between the bars of the stanchion. Jane closed them to keep her contained. She took a three-legged stool off the wall and sat down at the cow's side. After a few seconds, he heard milk splashing into the galvanized pail.

He moved to the far side of the cow and stroked her back. Jane had her face down. Danny couldn't see her expression. "Why me?"

"I saw you playing with the kids and a dog at your school. I took a chance that you were the right person to find her a home."

"Why didn't you ask me?"

She leaned back to look at him. "My uncle doesn't care for the Amish."

"That explains why your uncle didn't ask, not why you didn't."

"Maybe because I wanted to avoid this," she said dryly.

"A conversation over the back of a cow?"

"Exactly." She looked down, but not before he glimpsed her smile.

He wished he could see her face again. "All kidding aside, are you in trouble? I'm pretty good at reading children, one side effect of being a teacher. I can see Bridget is afraid of that man."

He waited, but she said nothing. "At least you don't deny it."

When she stood up, there were tears in her eyes. He felt like a heel. Her lip quivered an instant before she regained control. "My uncle is a stern man. I don't like to cross him. Neither should you. I'm glad you're willing to care for Holly. Thank you for that. Now I need to finish my chores and you need to leave."

She picked up her pail and hung her stool back on the wall. Danny couldn't let it go. "How did you get that bruise on your face?"

"I'm clumsy. I walked into an open cabinet door. Not that it is any of your business."

Helpless in the face of her stoicism, Danny racked his brain for a way to get through to her. "I'm sorry for prying, but I must know. Has he hit Bridget?"

"I need to feed the hogs. You know where the door is. I guess my uncle is right. The Amish do like to sneak around."

"I apologize again if I've offended you. What I said about Holly is true. You and Bridget are welcome to visit her anytime. I want you to know that if you ever need a friend, I'll be at the school."

He turned to get the pup. Holly sat beside the hay bale, weaving slightly. The poor thing had to be exhausted. He took off his coat, pulled the water bottles and jerky out of his bag. He poured some of the water in his hand and she lapped it eagerly. Then he settled the puppy inside the satchel and hung it over his neck. Slipping his coat on, he closed it around her and put the water bottles in his pockets.

Jane continued watching him warily. He left the plastic bag of jerky on the hay bale. "I don't have room for this. Put it to good use for Bridget."

Stepping out the back door, he closed it behind him, feeling like a failure and more convinced than ever that Jane and Bridget were living in an abusive situation.

What could he do?

With him gone, Jane finally took a deep breath. Why did he have to come back? Why did he have to sound so caring? She hugged herself to suppress a shiver. Danny had no idea what her uncle could do if he had discovered him in the barn.

If she ever needed a friend. That was almost funny. No, it made her angry. She'd needed a friend for years and there were none to be found. Danny Coblentz thought he could waltz in here after a few minutes of talking to her and decipher her life. His mistake. He couldn't help her.

One lesson from her former life she remembered well. The Amish didn't interfere in the affairs of outsiders. Be in the world but not a part of it. Separation from the world was what the Amish preached and lived every day. Danny talked a good story, but he couldn't do anything.

She turned to go but caught sight of the plastic bag he'd left and snatched it up not wanting her uncle to know anyone had been in the barn. The bag contained what looked like jerky. When she opened it, the spicy aroma of smoked meat made her mouth water.

Put it to good use for Bridget.

Tears gathered in Jane's eyes. He'd left food for Bridget. She covered her face with her hands and wept with gratitude.

Chapter Three

When Danny reached home, he found Maddie sitting on the porch steps with Sadie Sue. The yellow Lab mix belonged to his friend Michael Shetler, but she roamed the small community of New Covenant at will, often arriving at the schoolhouse as the children came out for recess. They didn't have school on Saturdays, so her appearance surprised him.

"Aren't you cold sitting out here, Maddie?"

"Nope." She leaned to the side to look behind him with a puzzled expression. "Willis said you had a new puppy. Sadie Sue and I want to see it."

"You mean this puppy?" Danny opened his coat and pulled out the tired little dog. She perked up immediately and began thumping her tail against his side.

Maddie jumped up and took the pup from his arms. "She's *wunderbar*. What's her name?"

"Holly. I need to get her something to eat and drink. We've had a long walk." Climbing the steps, he opened the door. Maddie put the pup down. Holly began investigating Sadie Sue who seemed unsure of the puppy's enthusiasm. Holly dropped into a playful pose with her rump in the air and barked at Sadie Sue. She didn't need more of an invitation. She bounded down the steps and the two of them were soon chasing each other around Danny's front yard.

He called Sadie Sue over to break up the romp not wanting Holly to get overexerted. The pup wasn't strong yet. Maddie scooped the puppy up and carried her into his house. Taking a seat on the floor with the puppy in her arms, Maddie waited while he got the food ready. Sadie Sue watched from a respectful distance.

After the puppy ate and drank her fill, she stretched out in the box he had by the stove and soon fell fast asleep. Maddie stroked her silky ear. "She's so soft. Where did you get her?"

"A little girl named Bridget gave her to me. She couldn't keep her anymore."

"That's sad. She must miss her."

The look in Bridget's eyes as she said goodbye to Holly stuck with him. "She misses her a lot."

Nor would he soon forget the fear in Jane's eyes. How could he help? Praying for them was a given, but he needed to do more.

* * *

The following morning, it didn't surprise Danny when Maddie came in after first light. "We don't have to leave for church yet, so I came to play with Holly. Is that okay?"

"Sure, but don't take her outside without a leash and don't get your Sunday dress dirty. I need to talk to your brother."

Leaving Maddie to entertain the pup, Danny walked to the road that ran through the village and crossed it. He found Willis inside enjoying a cup of coffee with Eva. The house held the lingering smell of bacon, fresh baked rolls and woodsmoke.

Eva got up to get Danny a cup. "We missed you at breakfast. Would you like a cinnamon roll before we leave for services?"

Sinking onto a chair beside Willis at the table, he nodded. "That would be *wunderbar.*"

"Did you find the owner of the dog?" Willis took a sip from his mug.

"I did. The woman and child live about three miles on the other side of Zook's farm."

"Did she have an explanation for leaving the puppy on your doorstep?"

Danny shook his head. "We didn't talk much. The owner of the farm ordered me off his land. Apparently, the man is their uncle."

Danny took a deep breath while he decided

how much to share. At his wit's end for how to help, he decided to give his brother-in-law all the details.

"Willis, they're afraid of him. The woman had a bruise on the side of her face I'm sure came from a slap. I left but then waited to talk to her later when she came into the barn to do chores. She says they're fine, but they aren't."

Eva put his coffee in front of him and sat down. "Why don't you believe her?"

"I saw how frightened they were when their uncle came out to confront me. When we were alone, I asked her point-blank if he ever hit Bridget. She didn't deny it."

"What are you going to do?" Willis asked.

Danny shrugged. "That's why I'm here. I'm hoping you can tell me how to help. They're *Englisch*. I can speak to our bishop, but I don't know what he can do. The woman understood Deitsh."

"Ex-Amish or perhaps Old Order Mennonite?" Eva suggested.

"That's what I thought." Danny stared into the steaming black coffee. "She wanted me to take the dog and leave. My arrival seriously upset her uncle. I gathered he doesn't like the Amish. What can I do? I can't leave them there."

Willis pulled on his short beard thoughtfully. "I don't like it any more than you do, but what choice do you have?"

"Pastor Frank Pearson will know what to do," Eva stated with surety.

Willis looked puzzled. "The Mennonite minister over at Fort Craig?"

Eva nodded. "He deals with people in crisis in his AA program and in his survivors' support group meetings. Pastor Frank is the person you should see."

Danny got up. "I can catch him at church today. *Danki*."

"You're going now?" Eva asked.

"This can't wait."

Eva followed him to the door. "Danny, be careful."

"Hey, I'm always careful on the road."

"I'm not talking about your driving. You know we're not to involve ourselves in the lives of outsiders. Consider what you're doing."

He took his sister's hand and squeezed. "If our *Englisch* neighbor's house caught fire, would you tell me to think before I ran to help? You didn't look into their eyes, sister. You didn't hear the rage in that man's voice."

She sighed and nodded. "All right. *Gott* go with you and don't be late for church."

Late on Tuesday morning, the shrill ring of the telephone startled Jane so much she jabbed herself with her sewing needle. Putting her finger in her mouth, she laid aside Bridget's torn dress and stared at the phone. Albert wasn't home. He'd gone with a friend to tear down a garage, one of the rare odd jobs he occasionally took.

The phone rang again. He didn't like her to answer it, so she waited for the machine to pick up. Maybe it was a wrong number.

The machine clicked on, and she heard a woman's voice. "This message is for Albert Newcomb. I'm Melissa Fredericks with the offices of Child and Family Services. This call is to inform you that I'll be making a child protection assessment visit tomorrow at ten a.m. if that time is convenient. If not, please call our office and reschedule or if you have any questions." The woman rattled off a number that Jane didn't catch.

Child and Family Services were coming here? Why?

The answer slammed into her brain. Danny had called them and done this. He couldn't leave well enough alone.

What did a child protection assessment entail? Jane clasped her hands together tightly. Could they take Bridget away from her? Albert had warned her that would happen if she ever complained about him. Her heart began pounding wildly. She couldn't lose Bridget.

If Danny had started this, he could stop it. He

could tell them his suspicions weren't true and there was no need for a visit. She had to see him.

Rushing up the ladder to the loft where Bridget was taking a nap, Jane pulled back the quilt. "Bridget, honey, you need to get up."

Bridget sat up rubbing her eyes. "I had a dream about Holly."

"That's exactly why you must get dressed. We're going to see Holly. Hurry up."

"We are really going to visit her?" Bridget grinned happily.

"If you get dressed."

"Okay." She jumped out of bed and began pulling on her pants. "I get to see Holly again. I'm so happy."

Jane didn't share her enthusiasm. She'd have to face Danny and convince him to call off the visit. He'd made things so much worse for her.

After bundling Bridget in her coat, Jane took the child's hand and walked briskly toward New Covenant under a low gray sky. Her breath rose in white puffs in the frigid air as she hurried.

Bridget tugged on her hand. "Auntie Jane, slow down."

"You want to visit Holly, don't you? We must hurry."

"Why?"

"Because she's sad without you. She misses you."

"But I'm getting tired." Bridget yanked her hand away.

Jane wanted to yell at her to keep going but realized pushing the child too hard wouldn't help. "I'll carry you for a while."

After settling Bridget on her hip, Jane trudged on. Fat snowflakes started falling around them. The sound of a car on the road behind her made Jane step off to the side. A battered green-and-white pickup stopped beside them. A middle-aged woman rolled down the window. "Do you need some help?"

Jane's reluctance to talk to strangers warred with her need to reach Danny. "We're going to the Amish school at New Covenant."

"I know right where that is. I'm Lilly Arnett, by the way. Get in and I'll give you a lift."

"We shouldn't," Bridget whispered in Jane's ear.

Jane set her on the ground. "It's okay this once."

Ten minutes later, the woman dropped them in front of the school. Jane waved her thanks and took Bridget's hand. Danny would fix this. He had to.

At the door to the school, she hesitated, but gripping Bridget's hand harder, she pushed open the door and went inside. A roomful of children turned in their seats to look. Bridget pressed close to her. Danny stood at the blackboard with his back toward her, writing something. She started forward as he turned around.

"Jane, what are you doing here?"

"Tell them not to come, Danny. You said you wanted to help but not this way." Her words tumbled over each other.

"Auntie Jane, you're hurting my hand."

She looked down at Bridget and fell to her knees filled with remorse. "I'm sorry. I didn't mean to. I'm so sorry, honey."

Tears began streaming down Jane's face. She looked up to see Danny towering over her. "Please, tell them not to come." She could barely get the words about between sobs. "I can't lose her."

Danny beckoned to one student and knelt beside Bridget. "I expect you want to see Holly, don't you?"

Bridget nodded but looked uncertain.

A girl a few years older than Bridget came to Danny's side. "Bridget, this is Maddie. She's going to take you over to play with Holly while I talk to Jane."

"Is that all right, Auntie Jane?" Bridget asked fearfully.

Jane nodded and tried to regain her composure. Danny smiled at the child. "She's at my house. Go with Maddie. It's all right."

The girls went out the door; Danny stood and

helped Jane to her feet. She grasped his arms, not sure her legs would hold her.

He looked around the room. "Class, you may all go out for recess now. Otto, please ask Eva to come here as soon as she can."

The children dispersed quietly but with curious glances at Jane. When they were outside, he led Jane to a bench at the back of the schoolroom. "Sit. I'm going to get some water."

Jane nodded, more exhausted than she had ever been in her life.

Danny walked to the front of the room, filled a glass from the water cooler and headed back to her. A woman rushed in breathlessly. Gesturing toward Jane, he handed the woman the glass and took a seat at a desk.

The smiling woman came and sat beside Jane. She handed her the water. "I'm Eva, Danny's sister. What's going on?"

The sympathy in Eva's eyes made Jane wish she could confide in her, but she couldn't trust anyone. Jane took a drink and struggled to regain her composure. "Danny can fix this. I'll only speak to him."

"Are you sure?"

Jane nodded and looked around fearfully. "Where's Bridget?"

"Playing with the puppy and my daughter. She's fine. Shall I have her come back?"

"Yes, please."

Eva went over to Danny. "She says is it's something you must fix. What did you do?"

"I have an inkling. *Danki* for coming so quickly."

"When Otto burst in to tell me a hysterical woman had collapsed on the school floor, I thought to make haste. Is she the one you talked about?"

"*Ja*, she's the one."

Jane dropped her head in shame. They had been discussing her. What had Danny told them?

"I'll take over the class. Do what you need to do." Eva went out.

Crossing the room, Danny pulled up a chair and sat facing Jane. "Can you tell me what's wrong?"

Anger surged to the surface as she focused on his face. Why would he do that? Why would he take her baby from her? "You betrayed me."

He met her gaze without flinching. "Tell me what's happened."

"Child and Family Services is making a child protection assessment tomorrow. They're coming to take my girl away from me. Because of you." She grabbed his arm. "Tell them you didn't mean it. There's nothing wrong and they don't have to come."

"You need to calm down, Jane," he said softly.

"How can I be calm when I'm going to lose

Bridget? Don't you understand? I can't lose her again. She's all I have."

"Child services may take her away from Albert, but they won't take her away from you. You're her aunt. She belongs with family."

A shaky laugh burst from Jane. He didn't understand how the system worked. "I have no home, no job, no way to provide for her. She'll be placed in foster care the way we both were before. Believe me, I know all about the foster care system."

"I don't understand."

Jane rubbed her temples, hating to dredge up those memories. "My parents died in a buggy and car crash a week after I turned seventeen. I went to stay with my only sister, Lois. She'd left our family and the Amish to study art. Lois wouldn't go back to the farm. She loved the city, her art, and she was pregnant but unwed. A few months after Bridget was born, Lois had a chance to study in Paris."

Lois had chosen art over her own child. From then on, Bridget became Jane's baby. The focus of her life. "Lois arranged for us to stay with our uncle, but she had to pay him to take us in. Not long after that, my sister died in France. The money stopped and Albert dumped us into foster care. They wouldn't let us stay together."

She had begged to keep Bridget, but the foster parents that took Jane in didn't want to care for an infant.

"They took her from my arms." Her voice trailed off. She stared at her clenched fingers as the worst day of her life replayed itself in her mind. The pain of that time still cut like a living thing, lashing her with grief and fear. It couldn't happen again. She wouldn't let it.

"I can't imagine the heartache you had to bear at such a young age," he said softly.

She looked up. "They separated us for six months, then Albert found out he could collect a stipend from the state for our care, and he took us back. The moment I had Bridget in my arms, I vowed we'd never be separated again. Never. Now will you stop their visit?"

He blew out a heavy sigh. "I never talked to anyone at child services. I talked to Pastor Frank Pearson. He's a minister in Fort Craig. Your uncle has done a few odd jobs for him. He knows Albert isn't exactly reliable and that he has a temper. The pastor contacted child services."

A bit of hope returned to her heart. "Then he can tell them it's a mistake."

Danny shook his head. "I don't know if they can cancel a visit. I'm to blame for this, but I have Bridget's best interest at heart. You say you are fine, but both of you are malnourished.

Your uncle is verbally if not physically abusive. No person should live like that."

Jane wanted to beat her fists against his chest. "I'm Bridget's best interest. She is my heart. We are fine as long as we're together."

"Jane, you aren't fine. Bridget isn't fine. Why can't you admit that?"

Because that meant she had failed in the most important task of all. Caring for her dead sister's baby.

She stood up. "I must get back. Uncle will be home soon."

Albert normally stayed out late on the days he collected his money, but she needed a reason to get away from Danny's probing.

His shoulders drooped and he nodded. "I'll drive you."

Spending more time in Danny's company filled her with dismay. "No. He can't see us together."

"At least let me take you partway so Bridget doesn't have to walk so far."

He was thinking of her child's welfare. She wanted to stay angry with him, but she couldn't. He had no idea the trouble he would cause by trying to do the right thing. "Okay but drop us off a half mile from the cabin."

In the buggy, Bridget chatted happily about her visit with Holly and her new friend Maddie.

Danny remained silent. The snow started coming down heavily, obscuring the forest around them. When he stopped the buggy to let them out, he looked at Jane with sad eyes. "I'm sorry. Perhaps things aren't as bad as I assumed. I pray the social worker will see that and make the right decision."

A faint hope, but all Jane had now. She'd do her best to present a picture of a poor but happy family tomorrow.

"If I can help in any way, know that I will." The kindness in his eyes touched something deep inside her. Something she had to ignore. Depending on someone else only led to heartache. She lifted Bridget out of the buggy. "You've helped enough."

He nodded sadly and turned the buggy around without another word.

Bridget skipped beside Jane as they walked toward the cabin. "Riding in a buggy is fun. Can we do it again the next time we visit Holly?"

"Maybe." Jane couldn't promise anything.

Thankfully, Albert's car wasn't in the yard when they reached home. But when she opened the cabin door, she found him waiting for them.

Jane's heart started pounding when she saw his livid expression. "Where have you been?"

Bridget pressed close. Jane nudged the child

behind her. "Go to the barn and give Mable some hay."

"Okay." Bridget scurried away.

Jane lifted her chin and walked to the kitchen table. She pulled off her hat and gloves and laid them down. "We went for a walk. Where is your car?"

"Wouldn't start when I left the bank. Had to bum a ride with a friend. There is a message on the answer machine."

He advanced on Jane. She cringed and stepped sideways to stay out of his reach. Stupid, stupid. In her panic, she hadn't deleted the message.

"About a job?" She tried to sound hopeful.

"No. Some busybody social worker is coming here. You turned me in, didn't you?"

"What? No, of course I didn't."

"You plan to tell them all about your mean uncle. You're going to have Bridget lie about me."

"Never. I'll tell them everything is fine. There's nothing to worry about."

He raised his hand. She put up her arms to block the blow, but he didn't strike her. He took a step back. "You'd like to show them a bruise, wouldn't you? You won't tell them anything because you won't be here. Get out. Now. Never set foot on this property again. I'll have you thrown in jail for trespassing so fast you won't know what hit you. Bridget will say what I tell her to say or else."

"I have nowhere to go."

"I don't care."

A strange calm filled Jane. Her life under Albert's threating shadow had ended. She was homeless. "I'll get my things."

"You brought nothing into this house. You'll take nothing out."

"I have my sister's sketchbook upstairs." And a few dollars she had scrounged over the summer recycling bottles and cans from the roadside. The book meant far more than the money. It meant everything to Bridget.

"Get out and be glad I'm letting you off easy. Or should I call the police?" He walked to the phone and picked up the receiver.

No money, only the clothes on her back in the middle of winter, where could she go? Jane's mind reeled. She focused on his face. He meant it.

Well, he was wrong about one thing. She had brought Bridget into this house. Jane wasn't leaving without her.

"I'll go. You'll never see me again."

She dashed out the door and headed to the barn as fast as she could run. Bridget stood petting Mable's broad nose. Jane skidded to a stop beside her. "Honey, we gotta leave. Right now. Come with me."

She heard the door of the house slam. "Bridget, get in here!"

Bridget's eyes grew wide with fright. "I should go."

"You never have to do anything he tells you again. We're leaving." Jane pulled the child toward the back door of the barn, taking only a moment to collect the plastic bag of jerky from under the hay where she had it hidden. Her hands shook so badly she almost dropped it.

"Bridget, don't you dare disobey me. Get out here right now." His voice sounded louder as he got closer to the barn. Jane pushed open the back door.

"Where are we going, Auntie Jane?"

"Away. As fast as we can."

Then what? It would be dark in a couple of hours. Snowflakes flew past on a stiff breeze signaling a coming storm as Jane headed into the woods. The road wouldn't be safe, but at least Albert didn't have a car to follow them. Could she outrun him?

Bridget stumbled in the deep snow. "I can't go so fast."

Jane picked her up. They needed shelter, but where?

Danny's kind eyes and his offer of help rose from her memory. Did she dare go to him? Or would he betray her?

Chapter Four

Seated at his kitchen table, Danny stirred a bowl of tomato soup with rice, usually one of his favorite meals. It didn't tempt him tonight. There were papers that needed grading, plans for the school Christmas program to complete, a yard to fence for his new puppy before the snow got too deep. Lots of things needed his attention, but his mind wasn't on any of them. Laying his spoon aside, he leaned back in his chair.

He'd made things worse for Jane. How much worse he didn't know, but he couldn't stop wondering. After dropping her near her uncle's cabin that afternoon, he'd gone straight to the phone shack near the school and called Pastor Frank, only to learn the social worker's visit to Albert's place couldn't be stopped. A complaint had to be investigated.

Holly whined near Danny's feet. He glanced

at the pup. "*Ja*, I messed up, but what else could I do? How was I to know they might take Bridget away from Jane?"

Maybe they wouldn't. Perhaps the situation wasn't as bad as she thought. True, Jane didn't have a job or a home for the child, but wouldn't the child welfare people help her secure those things? He wished he knew more about how the system worked. Among the Amish, outside help wasn't needed. The entire community cared for widows and orphans.

Folding his hands, he bowed his head. "Let them stay together, Lord. They need each other."

Holly sat up with her tail thumping rapidly. She darted to the front door and scratched at it.

"You just went out." Danny returned to stirring his soup.

The pup yipped, scratching harder.

"You'll ruin the wood, Holly. Stop it." Danny got up from the table.

The door flew open. Jane stumbled in amid a flurry of snow with Bridget in her arms. Ice crystals crusted their hair and clothes.

Jane slammed the door shut, keeping her back against it, then slowly sank to the floor. The color drained from her face. Her eyes closed, and her arms fell limply to her sides.

He kneeled beside her. "Jane, what happened?"

She didn't respond. Bridget scrambled off

Jane's lap and wrapped her arms around the squirming puppy trying to lick her face. "Holly, I'm so glad to see you."

Danny took Jane's ice-cold, limp hands in his own, rubbing them vigorously. Why wasn't she wearing gloves or a hat in this weather? "Jane, can you hear me? Speak to me."

She didn't move. He looked at Bridget. "What are you doing here?"

"I think we ran away."

"From Albert?"

Bridget nodded. "He started yelling for me to come into the house. Jane said I never had to obey him again. We ran out of the barn into the woods."

Danny patted Jane's pale cheek to revive her. "Jane, can you hear me? Jane, wake up."

Fear gripped his heart when she didn't respond. What was wrong? Was she hurt? He couldn't tell, but her breathing seemed shallow and fast.

Getting up, he grabbed an afghan from the sofa, draped it around her shoulders, then went to look out the window. Nothing moved in the winter twilight, but he couldn't see more than a dozen yards in the snow. "Did Albert follow you?"

"I don't know." Bridget moved to his side to

look out, too. "He's gonna be mad. He's mean to Jane when he gets mad."

Would he come here? Did he know where she'd gone? If not, the falling snow might cover any tracks she'd left.

Danny glanced with concern at Jane's pale face. Melting snow dripped from her hair. Using the corner of the throw, he dried her cold cheeks. Warmth was what she needed.

"Bridget, please get a quilt from the bed in the other room." Danny hurried to fill his kettle and put it on the stove.

Bridget returned, dragging the quilt behind her while the puppy jumped on and off before deciding on a tug-of-war game.

"Holly, no!" Bridget frowned at her. The puppy stopped and sat waiting for the next game to begin.

Danny quickly spread the quilt on the sofa. Then he pulled off Jane's footwear and wet socks. Her feet were like ice. He rubbed them briefly, glancing at her face, hoping it would rouse her. It didn't.

Peeling off her damp coat, he threw it aside, gathered her in his arms and carried her to the couch. Laying her down gently, he wrapped the quilt around her, tucking it under her bare feet. He pulled her long damp braid out from behind her and draped it over the arm of the sofa. Then he added more wood to the fire in the fireplace.

"Bridget, take your wet things off. Come here and get warm."

She shed her coat, then glanced at him with a troubled expression. "My clothes are wet, but I don't have any others."

Danny stepped into the bedroom and came out with a bathrobe. "Slip out of your things and wrap up in this. I'll be in the kitchen. Okay?"

She nodded.

At the stove, he pulled the steaming kettle off the heat. First, he needed to get something warm into Bridget, then get help for Jane. He emptied his untouched soup back into the pan to reheat.

"This is too big."

Bridget stood in the kitchen doorway with her arms outstretched. The sleeves dangled to her knees. Grinning, he beckoned her closer. "I can fix that."

He rolled up the material until her hands appeared. "There. How's that?"

"Okay. Something smells good." She stood on tiptoe to gaze at the stove.

"Do you like tomato soup?"

Her eyes widened. "Sure."

"It'll be ready in a minute. You can eat by the fire tonight." He scooped her up, carried her to his wingback chair, then pulled it closer to the fireplace. Holly jumped onto the chair with Bridget, snuggling down beside her. Glancing at Jane, he noted with relief some color returning to her pale cheeks.

Back in the kitchen, he filled a large mug half full of the warm soup. He carried it to Bridget and kneeled beside her. "I'm going to get my sister to help Jane. I won't be long."

"But what if Uncle Albert comes here?" Bridget whispered fearfully, sinking back into the depths of the chair.

Danny hated to leave her, but he had no choice. "I'll lock the door so he can't get in. You are not to answer if someone knocks. Understand?"

Her lower lip quivered, but she nodded. "I understand."

"I won't be long. Be brave." He chucked her under the chin. "I reckon I'll be back before you finish your soup."

That brought out a smile. "Promise?"

"I promise."

He checked on Jane. Her breathing had changed to slow and even. Grabbing his coat and hat, he took a flashlight from the kitchen drawer and went out, locking the door behind him.

The rising wind blew stinging snow into his face as he hurried toward the road. His torch barely penetrated three feet into the darkness and blowing snow, but he'd crossed this stretch of ground hundreds of times before. He reached his destination without trouble.

Stepping into his sister's kitchen, he slammed the door shut against the blustery wind, cutting off the sound of the storm. Willis and the children looked up from their places around the kitchen table.

Willis leaned back in his chair. "You missed supper, but I'm sure Eva can rustle something up for you. It's turning into a miserable night."

"Where is Eva? I need her help."

Willis frowned at the urgency in Danny's voice. "Nursing the baby. Maddie, go tell your mother that Danny's here. What's wrong?"

Maddie got up and hurried into the hallway off the kitchen.

Danny removed his hat and knocked the snow from it. "The woman who left the puppy on my doorstep just stumbled into my place and collapsed. The little girl is with her. I'm not sure what to do."

Eva came out ahead of Maddie. "Are they hurt?"

"Not that I can see. I wrapped Jane in one of my quilts and put her on the sofa. She needs to be out of her wet things."

Eva turned to Willis. "Ruth is sleeping now.

She shouldn't need anything for a few hours, but there's milk in a bottle in the refrigerator if she wakes before I get back."

He quickly came around the table and took her hands. "Don't worry about us. We'll manage."

Danny helped Eva into her overcoat. She wrapped a heavy gray wool scarf around her head and pulled on her gloves. "Do we need to take anything?"

"If you need something that I don't have, I'll come get it. We should hurry. I hated to leave the little girl alone."

Eva went out ahead of him. He held on to her arm as they trudged through the storm and deepening snow. Danny could barely discern the tracks he had made a few minutes earlier. If Albert didn't know where Jane and Bridget were, he'd have no hope of tracking them in this.

Danny unlocked the door. Holly sat up, barking sharply until she saw it was Danny. She licked Bridget's cheek and lay down again. Jane didn't stir.

"Bridget, this is my sister Eva. Are you done with your soup?" Danny hung up his coat and hat. Eva went straight to Jane's side.

"Last bite." Bridget ran her spoon around the edge of the bowl, licked it and held them out to him.

"Would you like some more?"

"No, thank you." Her bottom lip quivered as her voice cracked. "That's enough. Jane might want some when she wakes up."

Compassion squeezed his heart. Glancing at his sister, he saw the same emotion in her eyes. He took the bowl into the kitchen and returned with a second helping of soup and a slice of buttered bread on a plate.

"There's plenty for Jane. Don't worry about that."

"Really?" Bridget licked her lips but kept her hands tightly clenched.

"For sure and certain." He handed her the bowl, then pulled a side table close to her chair and placed the plate where she could reach it. "Now, don't let Holly eat your bread. She's already had her supper."

"I won't. It's really good. Thank you." Bridget's smile of gratitude was heartbreaking.

He'd never eat tomato soup again without remembering it. "Eva, what do you need me to do?"

Eva began unbraiding Jane's hair. "Get some towels. Bring me a pair of your flannel pajamas. It'll take too much time to go get mine. She's still cold. Do you have a hot water bottle?"

"Somewhere." If he could remember where

he'd stashed it. "There's hot water in the kettle already."

"*Goot*. Get the clothes first and then see if you can find that bottle. Oh, and put a couple of towels in the oven on low heat. When they're warm, I'll use them to cover her head and her hair."

"Is Jane okay?" Bridget asked in a small, fearful voice.

Eva smiled at her. "She'll be fine."

His sister sounded confident, but when Danny met her eyes, he knew she wasn't.

Deliciously warm and comfortable, Jane resisted opening her eyes. The soothing, familiar crackle of a fire and the smell of woodsmoke made her burrow a little deeper in the covers, but the movement triggered a multitude of aches. What had she done to earn them?

She managed to free her hand from the covers to reach for Bridget. The child always slept close, as much for comfort as for warmth. Feeling only empty space caused a sliver of concern to puncture Jane's serenity. Where was Bridget?

Jane opened her eyes. This wasn't their bed in the loft. It was a sofa. Where was she? Where was Bridget?

Albert's anger, her split-second decision to run, the bitter cold and the struggle through the woods. It all came rushing back. She sat bolt upright. "Bridget!"

Frantically, she searched the dark, unfamiliar room and tried to throw off the covers swaddled around her. Where was her child? Did Albert have her? No! Not after all she had done to get away. "Bridget, where are you?"

A figure rose from a nearby chair. Jane cringed against the sofa back.

"It's all right," he said. "She's sleeping in the other room. You're both safe."

With his back to the fire, Jane couldn't see his face, but she knew that voice. "Danny?"

"*Ja*, it's me. Give me a second, and I'll light the lamp."

"I need to see Bridget." Jane struggled with the cocoon of quilts around her. Something fell over her face. She pulled it away. Was it a towel? Her fingers discovered her wet hair underneath.

A second later, soft light filled the room. Danny lowered the glass chimney of a kerosene lamp on the table beside the sofa with a tiny clink. Holding the lamp aloft, he nodded toward a closed door. "She's in here."

Jane tried to get up and immediately fell back. Her shaky legs refused to hold her. Danny moved beside her in an instant. Grasping her arm, he helped her stand. The wooden floor felt cold on her bare feet.

"Are you okay?" His concern surprised her.

"Fine. Let me see Bridget."

"Sure." He guided her across the room, opened the door and held the lamp higher. Bridget lay curled on her side under a mound of quilts. She had one arm out around the puppy. Holly raised her head briefly but then settled back.

Her baby was safe. Jane's legs buckled and she fell against Danny. He caught her with his free arm and held her tight. "Easy does it. Can you make it to the sofa?"

"I think so."

"Put your arm around me."

Holding on to him, she made her way back to the couch and sank gratefully onto the cushions. A shiver rocked her.

Setting the lamp on the table, he lifted her legs to the sofa. "Back under the covers. That's an order."

Jane realized she wasn't wearing her clothes. The blue flannel fabric must be pajamas? Heat rushed to her face. "How did I get into these?"

"My sister was here until a few minutes ago. She dressed you in dry things."

"I don't remember."

Stepping back, he rubbed his hands on his pants. "I'm not surprised. You were out of it. Exhausted. Bridget told me you ran away."

Jane nodded slowly. Getting away from Albert had seemed like the most important thing, but now what?

Danny crossed his arms and stared at the floor. "I'm sorry for causing you so much trouble."

He looked up. "Are you hungry? Would you like some soup? Bridget ate the last of the tomato with rice, but I've got chicken noodle on the stove."

"That sounds good." Jane pulled back her damp hair. She found the towel she had tossed aside on the arm of the sofa and wrapped it around her head, turban-style.

Danny went into the kitchen. Jane pulled the covers up to her neck. She'd never felt so vulnerable in her life. Would he tell Albert where she was? Or would he help her escape with Bridget?

Escape to where?

No clothes, food, money. Nowhere to live or a way to earn a living. How could she take care of Bridget? Had she made a mistake? At least with Albert, Bridget would have a roof over her head.

Jane pulled the covers tighter. Now what?

"Here you go." Danny walked into the room, carefully balancing a tray. He put it on the small table beside his chair and then pulled it over to Jane. "I only have paper napkins. Sorry."

Jane stared at his offering. A white crockery bowl held a steaming concoction of thick noodles with big chunks of chicken and vegetables. The mouthwatering aroma pushed her worries to the back of her mind. A matching plate held two slices of homemade bread slathered with butter and strawberry jam. A full tumbler of milk stood beside the plate. She looked at Danny. "You should save some of this for Bridget."

"She had plenty to eat earlier. When she wakes up, she can have more."

"Don't you want any?"

"*Nee.* You go ahead." He hooked a thumb toward the kitchen. "I'm going to make coffee. Will you drink some?"

"Coffee sounds wonderful." Jane sat up and stared at the feast meant for her alone. She couldn't remember the last time she'd had a full bowl of soup and two slices of bread.

Lifting the spoon, she then savored the first sip of broth. Hearty, hot, perfectly salted and brimming with the flavor of cooked chicken, it was the most amazing thing she'd ever eaten. She took a second spoonful, closed her eyes and smiled. Pure bliss.

After that, she dove into the meaty bits of chicken, carrots, celery and thick noodles that reminded her of her grandmother's cooking. When she finished, she used a slice of bread to sop up every morsel from the bowl and gobbled it down. Picking up the second slice, she tore it in two and stuffed the first half in her mouth.

A sound from the kitchen made her look up. Danny stood in the doorway watching her with a box of crackers in his hand. Embarrassed, she reluctantly put the bread aside. She must look like a starving dog hunkered over her food. Picking up the glass of milk, she took a small sip.

He came into the room and set the box on her table. "I thought you might want some to go with your soup. Coffee's almost ready."

"Thank you."

When he returned to the kitchen, she grabbed a handful of crackers, wrapped them in a napkin and looked for a place to hide them. She stuffed them under a throw pillow, changed her mind and pushed them under the bottom of the sofa. Sitting up quickly, she wavered with dizziness and pressed a hand to her forehead.

"Are you okay?" Danny asked from the kitchen door.

"Woozy. It's passing."

Please, don't notice the napkin.

"I'll get you some water." He returned to the kitchen.

Jane bent down and pushed the crackers farther underneath his couch. Sitting up again, she put her head back and covered her eyes with her arm.

"Drink this."

Even in the lamplight, she read the deep concern on his face as he leaned over her. He was a handsome man. The sort of fellow she and her friends at school had giggled over and dreamed about marrying when they grew up.

Before her dreams crumbled into nothingness with the deaths of her parents and her harsh existence with Albert.

Taking the glass of water, she gulped it, ashamed to be hiding food from this kind man, but kindness wouldn't last. Nothing good lasted in Jane's world except Bridget.

They needed to move soon. Having more food would help. They weren't far enough away from Albert. Not yet.

Chapter Five

Danny pulled his chair over and sat facing Jane. The little house was quiet except for the crackling of the fire and the moaning of the wind outside. Jane looked frail and exhausted as she huddled in the red-and-white star quilt his sister had stitched for him.

"Jane, what happened tonight?"

She pushed a damp strand of hair away from her face. "Would you have a brush or a comb I can use?"

If she didn't want to talk to him, he wouldn't push her. "My sister used it on Bridget's hair before putting her to bed. I'll get it."

Jane reached for him. "Don't wake her."

"I won't." Stepping inside his bedroom, he located the brush on his bedside table. Bridget and Holly slept peacefully. Back in the living room, he started to close the bedroom door.

"Can you leave it ajar? I want to hear if she wakes. I don't want her to be scared in a strange place."

"Sure." Leaving the door open a few inches, he crossed the room to Jane and handed her the brush.

"Thanks." She took it and began dragging the brush through her tangles. She winced several times, then let her arms drop to her lap.

"Tired?"

"Yes."

"Would you like me to do it?"

She frowned at him. "Can you?"

He understood her confusion. Amish women kept their hair covered and never cut it, believing it was their crowning glory to be seen only by their husband and God. They never displayed their hair for vain reasons, but hair had to be washed and brushed out.

"I've seen my sister's and my mother's hair down hundreds of times and helped both when I couldn't think of an excuse to get outside. Little did I know it was *goot* practice for me. Maddie fell in a puddle last fall and ended up with her head caked in mud. My sister wasn't home, so I shampooed her. Another day at school Sarah's little brother put glue in her hair. I had to wash it before it dried. All in a day's work for a teacher, so I know how to use a hairbrush. Lie down. Rest your eyes."

He helped get her legs up, then held her hair as she lay back with her head on the arm of the sofa, allowing her hair to hang off the side. Pulling his chair around, he separated her hip-length sable-colored locks into three strands, working his way up each one to get the tangles out.

"You forgot to mention you brush your horse's tail." Her voice sounded tense.

"It crossed my mind, but I decided it wasn't the most flattering comparison."

That earned him a tiny smile and cheered him. "Tell me if I'm hurting you."

"You aren't."

He worked his way up to her scalp using long, slow strokes. She started to relax.

"Bridget said the two of you ran away."

Jane tensed. "Do you think she's warm enough?"

"I'm sure she is." He stopped brushing. "Do you want it braided, or shall I leave it loose?"

"You can braid hair, too?"

"I can manage."

Raising her hand, she felt along the length of one strand. "It's still damp. I'll leave it loose."

"All right. I tried to get the welfare visit stopped, Jane. I called Pastor Frank after I dropped you off.

He said a complaint of abuse and neglect had to be investigated."

She gazed into space. "I should have erased the message on the machine. I was too upset to think. When I got back to the cabin, Albert had already listened to it. He was furious, accused me of reporting him. Then he told me to get out."

"And Bridget?"

"She would say whatever he told her to say if I wasn't there to make her lie." Jane pulled the quilt up and closed her eyes. "I'm tired."

"So you took Bridget and ran."

"He'll tell the police I kidnapped her." She pressed a hand to her mouth and looked at Danny with fear-filled eyes. "I shouldn't have said that. You can't tell anyone I'm here."

"I won't. Relax."

She drew a shaky breath. "If they find me, I'll go to jail. Bridget won't have anyone to protect her. How could I be so—stupid?" Her voice trailed off.

Danny saw her exhaustion. "You're both safe tonight. The storm will keep Albert away until it blows over. Get some rest. We'll think of what to do next in the morning."

"You're helping a criminal." Her eyes closed and her head tipped slowly to the side.

"That's not the way I see it." Danny pulled the quilt up to her chin. She didn't stir.

He sat back in his chair and gazed at her. She was in serious trouble. He had no idea how to help. This went beyond anything he'd encountered before. Eva would be back soon. Maybe she would know what to do.

He dozed in his chair after that. The sound of his front door opening made him sit up and rub his face. Eva came in, brushing the snow from her coat. "How are they?"

After glancing at Jane, he joined his sister by the front door. "Sleeping. Jane woke and ate a little."

"*Goot.* She's much too thin and so is that poor child. What will you do now?"

"They can't stay here."

"That's obvious. Willis and I talked it over. We'd like them to stay with us."

Danny wanted to throw his arms around his bighearted sister. "*Danki.* That's *wunderbar.* I need to sort out how to keep them safe."

Eva put her hand on his shoulder. "You feel responsible for them. I understand that, but they aren't Amish. Pastor Frank will help them."

"He can't know they're here, Eva."

Her eyebrows shot up. "Are you serious? Why not?"

"Jane believes Albert will have told the police

she kidnapped Bridget. She will be arrested if she's found."

Eva frowned. "Pastor Frank won't allow that."

"I don't want to take the risk and neither does Jane."

"*Brudder*, she can't hide forever."

Danny sighed heavily. "I know. There must be a way to keep them together."

Eva glanced around him to where Jane slept on the sofa. "The Lord will show us what needs to be done. We must accept His will even if it isn't what we want. For now, Jane and Bridget need to regain their strength. We must offer what comfort we can. I'll get started on breakfast. You need to get ready for school. Maddie tells me everyone is excited to begin practicing for their Christmas program."

"I almost forgot. I need to choose a play for the *kinder* today."

Eva pressed her lips together, then blurted out, "Let them choose it this year."

Danny wasn't sure what she was getting at. "Didn't you like the program last year?"

"It was—fine."

"Not quite a glowing review."

"Fishing for compliments, *brudder*?"

"Of course not." Still, his sister could have said something nice. "The children worked hard to learn those songs and poems."

"It showed. They did an excellent job."

"Then what was wrong with it?"

"I said it was fine."

"But it was the way you said it." He pressed for more details. "Tell me."

Eva folded her arms over her chest. "A sprinkling of humor would be nice this year."

"Humor?"

"*Ja*, that special something that makes us smile and laugh."

"I know what humor is."

"Really, because I couldn't tell from last year's program."

"It's up to me to choose what's appropriate. I'm the teacher."

"Have faith in your scholars. Let the *kinder* look over the plays and skits. I'm sure they'll find something that's fun and suitable. Offer to let them write something."

Danny stared at the floor. Should he? The children would love the idea. He glanced at his sister. "Was it boring?"

"Not boring but not stirring. Do you know what I mean?"

"You think Maddie and Otto can plan a better program? What if she wants to give her imaginary friend Bubble a part?"

Eva laughed. "Bubble hasn't appeared in

ages, but don't give up your oversight. Go get ready. I'll have breakfast in fifteen minutes."

Danny quietly got his clothes from his room. Bridget didn't stir, but Holly got down to follow him. He let her outside and watched as she frolicked in the new snow. He would have to put a fence around the yard if he was going to keep her. Sadie Sue might wander around the settlement, but he didn't trust Holly to do the same. Sadie Sue had been a stray and was used to looking after herself until she found his friend Michael Shetler and decided to look after him.

Holly bounded up the steps to come back in. Danny scanned the road and the forest edge. He didn't see any sign of Albert.

Once inside, Holly headed toward the kitchen. Eva had the pup's breakfast ready. Ten minutes later, when Danny stepped out of the bathroom, Holly was nowhere in sight. Danny took his place at the kitchen table. "Where's the dog?"

"She wanted back in with Bridget. It's going to be hard to separate those two."

"Maybe we won't have to."

Eva planted her hand on her hip and pointed her spatula at him. "I will take in Jane and Bridget, but I refuse to have a dog in my house."

"Okay. I'll keep her, but only until Bridget and Jane are somewhere safe. The dog belongs with them."

He wolfed down his toast and scrambled eggs, then with a glance at Jane still sleeping on his sofa, he went out the door to face another day at the best job he'd ever had.

Most of his students were already playing on the school grounds. The heavy snow hadn't kept them away. After counting heads, he realized only Annabeth Beachy hadn't arrived. The jingle of sleigh bells made him look toward the road. Tully Lange drove up in his sleigh with his stepdaughter seated between him and his wife, Becca. Everyone's cheeks were rosy from the cold. The black horse snorted, sending a cloud of vapor into the air.

Annabeth hopped out. *"Guder mariye, Teacher."*

"We only speak English at school," Danny reminded her. Amish folks spoke Pennsylvania Dutch or Deitsh at home. Children learned English once they started school.

"I forgot. Good morning, Teacher. Hi, Maddie." Annabeth waved at her friend and hurried toward her.

Danny patted the horse's shoulder. "Morning, Tully, Becca, it's nice to see you."

"Did all the children get here?" Tully asked.

"Everyone's accounted for."

Becca smiled. *"Goot*, and how is your new puppy?"

Danny refrained from looking toward his house. He could feel heat rising up his neck. "Fine."

Tully tipped his head slightly. "What's wrong? You look beat."

"Nothing's wrong," Danny said quickly. He glanced toward the house. How could he keep Jane's and Bridget's presence a secret from his friends and the children at the school? It would be impossible.

Tully chuckled. "She kept you up last night, didn't she?"

"What?" Danny looked at his friends in shock. How could they know about his company?

"Make sure she gets plenty of exercise in the evening. It will help her sleep," Becca said.

Danny realized they were talking about the puppy. His guilty conscience would give him away if he wasn't careful. "Sounds like *goot* advice. *Danki*."

Tully and Becca drove away. Danny went inside. He had a few minutes before it was time to call the children in. Taking out a catalog, he turned to the pages listing Christmas plays and started reading the descriptions of each one. There were two dozen plays he could pick from or, if he did as Eva suggested, he could have the children choose something.

How could he get fourteen children to all agree on one play?

The outside door opened. Maddie and Annabeth came in. The girls went into the cloakroom to hang up their coats. He glanced at the clock and headed to the front door and the bell rope hanging beside it. Grasping the rope, he rang the bell and then held open the door for the children to come in.

Maddie came over. "How is Holly this morning?"

"She's fine." Clearly Eva hadn't told her about Jane and Bridget's arrival.

"Won't she be lonely all day with you at school?"

"I'll go home at lunch time and check on her." He wanted to rush home now and discover how Jane and Bridget were getting on, but Eva would have things well in hand. He trusted his sister.

Moving to the front of the classroom, he sat on the corner of his desk. The tall windows of the school normally gave him a clear view across the lawn to his front porch, but this morning they were covered in sparkling patterns of frost.

How was Jane? Was she up yet? Had she and Bridget gone to Eva's home? What could he do to help Jane other than give her refuge?

As soon as all the students had quietly taken

their seats, Danny moved to the blackboard that covered the front wall. He wrote out the date and the arithmetic assignments for each of the grades. When he finished, he picked up his Bible. This morning he chose Proverbs 8:32-33.

"'Now therefore harken unto me, O ye children: for blessed are they that keep my ways.

"'Hear instruction, and be wise, and refuse it not.'"

After the reading, his students rose, clasped their hands together and recited the Lord's Prayer in unison. Then they filed to the front and lined up by grades to sing. Instead of telling them what songs he'd chosen for the day, Danny picked up the catalog. If he trusted his sister, he needed to heed her advice.

"We are going to choose a play and a skit for our Christmas program today. I'm going to have the eighth grade students choose from the ones listed here."

Otto didn't look thrilled, but Sarah Miller and Candace King looked ready to burst with excitement.

He prayed they wouldn't get carried away. "Keep the younger children in mind when you are deciding." Hope Crump and Matthew Brenneman were his first grade students. Sarah's younger brother Isaac was in the third grade.

"Can't we help pick a play?" Annabeth asked.

"The younger grades are going to decide on our songs. Middle grade scholars are going to choose several poems."

Enoch King folded his arms over his chest. "I don't like poetry."

His sister Candace gave him a playful bop on the head. "You don't have to like it—you just have to learn it."

Enoch stuck out his tongue at his sister. Danny grimaced. Hopefully, the children would come to an agreement and things would progress smoothly. "Let's sing 'Joy to the World' now. We'll split into groups after, and you may discuss what you want to present for our program."

Bridget's cheerful chatter pulled Jane awake. She lay still, listening to her explain to Holly that they had to be quiet. "When Auntie Jane wakes up, she'll read us a story from my mommy's special picture book. But we can't wake her. Eva says she needs her rest. If you disobey, you won't get any breakfast."

Jane winced as she recalled the many times Bridget had been forced to forgo a meal over some imagined infraction. Holly whined. Jane didn't know if the puppy was agreeing to or opposing the restriction.

"You are such a good dog. That's why I love you." Bridget clearly thought the puppy understood the rule.

Jane sat up. "Puppies and little girls deserve breakfast every day."

"You're awake." The child launched herself into Jane's arms. "Isn't this a wonderful house? I'm so glad Holly gets to live here. I hope she never has to go back to Uncle Albert's."

Jane tightened her arms around Bridget. "Holly never has to go back to and neither do we."

"Really?"

That one word, filled with so much hope, almost broke Jane's heart. "Truly. No matter what it takes, you won't go back."

Maybe she didn't have the right to make that promise, but Bridget deserved to be worry-free as long as possible.

"Holly wants to hear a story, but I can't find my picture book. I told her about my favorite Christmas one with the new baby."

It was the story of Bridget's birth. The book was lost forever unless Jane could figure a way to get it without Albert knowing. That didn't seem possible. As much as she wanted to recover the book, it wasn't worth risking Bridget's freedom to get it. "I'll tell you the story later.

Perhaps you can draw your own pictures. Would you like that?"

Bridget shook her head. "No, Mommy drew all the pictures for me."

"Are you ready for some breakfast?" Eva stood in the kitchen doorway.

"Am I?" Bridget asked Jane under her breath. She still worried that her food would be taken away.

Jane tickled the child's ribs making her giggle. "I don't know about you, but I'm starved. I'm sure Eva has fixed something delicious."

"If scrambled eggs, sausage patties and brown sugar and cinnamon oatmeal qualify, then that is exactly what you can have."

Bridget's eyes lit up, but she didn't move out of Jane's embrace.

Jane set her on the floor and gave her a little push toward the kitchen. "I can't get up until you get off my lap, Bridget. Hurry before it gets cold."

Bridget didn't need further urging. She rushed past Eva, and Jane heard her exclamation of delight. "Jane, there's loads of food."

Jane stood up. The room swirled around her. She sat down abruptly and after a moment, the dizziness passed.

Eva walked over with a steaming cup of coffee in her hands. "I sweetened this with honey.

You need the energy after your ordeal. Don't get up until you are feeling fully recovered. I'll bring your breakfast tray in here."

"I don't want to be a bother."

Eva chuckled. "I'll let you know the moment you become too much trouble."

"Where is Danny?"

"At school."

"Is it still snowing?" Jane took a sip of the coffee.

"It stopped about an hour ago. I think the storm is over for now."

That meant Albert would be looking for them. Jane tossed the quilt aside as fear set her heart pounding. "We need to get going."

"Are you sure? At least have something to eat."

"Bridget and I have to leave." She lowered her voice so Bridget couldn't overhear. "My uncle can't find us."

"I'm sorry you're in this horrible situation. Families are supposed to help one another. My husband will hitch up the sleigh and take you wherever you want to go."

She had nowhere to go. Jane's burst of energy vanished. Tears welled up in her eyes.

Eva took the coffee cup from her trembling hand. "Danny and I talked it over. We think you and Bridget should stay with my family for a while. Until things are settled."

"Are you offering us a place to stay?"

"I am."

"Why?"

"Because it's the right thing to do."

It had been a long time since anyone had shown her kindness. Did she dare trust this woman? A stranger?

Eva's gaze softened. "Our Lord commands us to care for those in need. Unless I miss my guess, you and Bridget qualify as needy. That isn't a bad thing. We all require assistance at some time in our life. It is prideful to deny you need help, although I'll admit that giving charity is easier than accepting it. Still, the Lord sets our feet on our path and only He knows why."

Jane sank onto the sofa. She didn't have a choice. For Bridget's sake, she would have to accept this woman's offer. "I'll repay you when I'm able."

Eva looked toward the kitchen. "Seeing that child happy and healthy will be payment enough."

"If my uncle or the police find me, you could be in trouble."

"Why would they look for you among us Amish folk?"

"Because I used to be Amish."

"Did you?" Eva smiled. "Where are you from?"

"I grew up in a community in New York."

"Then you have kin there?"

Jane shook her head. "My family is gone except for my uncle and Bridget."

"Danny is determined to find somewhere safe for you to go. Can you think of anyone who might take you in back in New York?"

"Maybe. I'm not sure." Could she beg shelter from some people her parents had known even if she wasn't Amish anymore? Albert might expect her to go there, but without money or the means of earning any, she couldn't travel that far except by hitchhiking. That would be impossible to do with Bridget in the winter.

Eva patted her arm. "Well, don't worry. Danny will think of something."

"Albert knows I gave Holly to Danny. He has seen him. He'll come here or send the police."

Eva tipped her head as she considered Jane's assertion. "Does your *onkel* know Danny is our teacher or where he lives?"

Jane thought back over her conversation with Albert. "I never mentioned it."

"Then he isn't likely to appear here today. Now, put your feet up while I go get your breakfast. You need to regain your strength. When you are feeling strong enough, we'll walk over to my house together." Eva returned to the kitchen.

Jane settled back on the sofa. Had her uncle already reported her to the police? It would have been easy for him to make a phone call. The social worker would arrive today. What would he tell her? How soon before the police began to question the Amish in New Covenant, and someone mentioned the schoolteacher had a new puppy? Days? Hours? Once Albert learned that he'd be at Danny's door.

Jane needed somewhere to hide with Bridget. Would they be safe across the road with Eva?

The smell of cooking sausage made Jane's stomach rumble. Eva was right. Jane needed to regain her strength if she had any hope of escaping. She pulled the quilt to her chin but kept an uneasy eye on the front door.

Chapter Six

After a wonderfully satisfying breakfast while snuggled under a warm quilt, Jane's determination to remain vigilant became a failing struggle. She kept nodding off and jerking awake. Her eyes grew heavier by the minute.

Bridget crawled onto the sofa with her. "I'm tired. Can you read me a story from Momma's book?"

How to tell her the beloved sketchbook was gone forever? It was so unfair. "Not now, sweetheart. I'm tired, too."

"Okay." Bridget settled under the quilt and was soon asleep, sandwiched in the crook of Jane's arm. Was there some way to recover the sketchpad? The thought of confronting Albert made a rock of fear settle in her midsection. She couldn't go back there.

Holly returned to the box by the stove. In the

warm, quiet house, a sense of security enveloped Jane, but she resisted giving in. It wasn't
real. There was no safe haven. Bridget could rest
for a minute more, then they needed to leave.

Eva kneeled beside Jane, startling her out of
her doze. "It's all right. It's just me. I have a
new baby that needs my attention at home, but
I won't be long."

Jane tried to sit up. Eva stopped her with a
hand on her shoulder. "Let the child rest, and
you do the same."

Jane stared at Eva in wonder. This stranger
had put aside the needs of her family to care for
Jane and Bridget. Jane barely remembered when
people behaved so unselfishly. "Thank you for
everything you've done."

"You're welcome. I'll lock the door. Danny
has a key and so do I. Your clothes are almost
dry. I left them hanging by the kitchen stove.
I'll be back soon, and I'm sure Danny will come
while the children are having their lunch break."

Hearing his name lifted Jane's flagging spirits. He had saved her and Bridget, given them
sanctuary, fed them, even turned over his bed to
Bridget while he spent the night in a chair. His
kindness and that of his sister boggled Jane's
mind. She owed them more than she could ever
repay.

Of all the people in New Covenant she might

have left Holly with, God had directed her to Danny. It was almost as if He still cared about her, but Jane had stopped believing that a long time ago.

When Eva left, Jane tightened her arms around the sleeping child and stroked Bridget's soft red hair. Had she been foolish to take her away from the only home she knew? Wasn't Albert's thoughtless care better than starving in the woods?

No, she had to believe this was the right decision. They were safe now, but for how long?

She closed her eyes. "Please, God, if you're listening, protect this child."

Holly woofed, scrambled out of her box and sat by the door. Jane's heart jumped and hammered painfully. Was it Albert? She heard a key turn in the lock. The door opened slowly.

"Do you need out?" Danny whispered to the groveling pup. She woofed again.

"Shh, come on." Holly slipped out. Danny went out with her. Jane's wildly beating heart gradually calmed. A few minutes later, the door opened again. He looked in. Seeing her awake, he smiled. "I hope I didn't disturb you."

She touched her finger to her lips and pointed to the child snuggled on her chest. He nodded, closed the door quietly and came in.

"How are you?" he whispered.

"Better."

"Glad to hear it. Where's my sister?"

"Gone home to take care of her baby. She said she would be back soon."

"Are you up to taking a short walk? Eva lives across the road. I think you'll be more comfortable there."

"And she won't have to leave her baby to come take care of us. I'm sure I can make it. I need to get dressed." She gently shook Bridget.

The child sat up rubbing her eyes. "I fell asleep."

"You did." Jane smiled at her. "We're going to stay at Eva's house."

Bridget frowned. "But I like it here. Holly lives here. I want to stay with her."

Danny leaned forward. "You can come visit as often as you like. Do you remember Maddie?"

Bridget nodded. "She's a nice girl."

"Her oldest brother, Willis, is married to Eva. Maddie, her brother's Harley and Otto all live with them."

"Why don't they live with their parents?"

"Because their parents have gone to be with God."

"Like my mommy?"

His eyes filled with sympathy. "That's right. Maddie will enjoy having you stay with her. I'm sure the two of you will have lots of fun. Eva has a new baby, too. Her name is Ruth."

Bridget turned to cup Jane's cheek, her eyes brimming with concern. "You're coming with me, aren't you, Auntie Jane?"

Jane kissed Bridget's palm. "Of course I am."

Bridget relaxed. "Because we belong together."

"Absolutely right," Jane assured her. "It's cold out. We need to get dressed. I can't go outside in these pajamas. You can't go out in that nightgown."

Bridget chuckled. "Nope. We sure can't."

Danny stood. "I'd better get back to school. Sarah Miller is my oldest pupil and an excellent teacher's helper, but I don't like to leave the *kinder* unsupervised for long."

Bridget tipped her head to the side. "What are *kinder*?"

Danny tweaked her nose. "Children like you. That's an Amish word."

"Kinder." Bridget smiled at Jane. "I learned a new word today. Can I go to school, too, Jane?"

"When you're a little older." Jane hoped someday Bridget would have a real home and go to school like other children. And not live in fear.

She got to her feet, discovering aches from

head to toe. "Eva said my clothes were in the kitchen."

"I'll get them for you." Danny left the room.

Bridget's coat and mittens were hanging over the back of the chair near the fireplace. They were dry to the touch. Jane picked them up and opened the bedroom door. When she turned around, Danny was standing behind her. He held out her bundle of clothes.

Her hand brushed his as she took them from him. A jolt of awareness sent a tingle up her arm and caused her to jerk away. He took a step back and rubbed his hands on his pants. Had he felt it, too?

"I'm sure Eva will return soon. It's probably best you don't go outside alone."

Jane nodded in unspoken understanding. Albert might be looking for them.

Danny turned on his heel and hurried out the door, locking it. Holly whined and scratched at the door wanting to follow.

"Come here, Holly." Bridget clapped her hands. The pup hurried over. Bridget gathered the dog in her arms and hugged her. "She'll miss us, Auntie Jane."

"We won't be far away." Not yet, but they would have to leave New Covenant soon. The community was too small to hide from Albert for long. Jane hated depending on the kindness of strangers, but she had no choice for now. Extracting the crackers from beneath the sofa, she stuffed them in her pocket.

Danny left the school as quickly as his dismissed students that afternoon. He couldn't wait any longer to check on Jane and Bridget. Despite his confidence that Eva would make Bridget and Jane comfortable in her home, he couldn't shake the feeling they were his responsibility. His interference had led Jane to flee Albert's home in desperation.

When he stepped outside the school, he saw a state police car drive past on the highway. The trooper didn't stop or even slow down. Was he looking for Bridget and Jane? How soon before the police started questioning the locals?

Danny hurried across the snow-covered lawn and found his front door unlocked. That told him Eva had taken his guests to her place. Inside the house, Holly greeted him joyfully, frisking around his feet, but the place seemed empty.

The unexpected sensation surprised him. He lived alone, but the house had never seemed so quiet before. He left the papers he needed to grade on the kitchen table and bent down to fill Holly's food bowl.

A knock at the door startled him. He opened

it cautiously. "Pastor Frank. What are you doing here?"

Frank looked perplexed. "You wanted to know how Albert Newcomb's child welfare visit went today. At least that's what you led me to believe."

"Oh right. I've had a busy day. Come in. How did it go?" He stepped aside so the minister could enter. He wasn't willing to lie, but he didn't have to share what he knew about Jane's situation. Had Albert reported Bridget's kidnapping?

Frank was smiling. "Your worry was for nothing."

That surprised Danny. "Really? Everything is okay?" How was that possible?

"The child wasn't at home. She and her aunt are visiting some friends out of state. The welfare visit was rescheduled for two weeks."

"Oh." Why hadn't Albert reported Bridget and Jane missing? Why make up a story about them visiting family? Jane needed to know this.

Frank's eyes narrowed. "Is everything all right, Danny? You seem distracted."

"I'm fine, except Eva convinced me to let the students choose their own play and skits for the Christmas program. I'm worried about what they'll decide on."

Pastor Frank grinned. "I'm sure it will be a

delightful program, no matter what the children choose."

Danny chuckled and leaned one shoulder against the doorjamb, trying to appear relaxed. "As long as Bubble doesn't make a reappearance."

Frank's grin widened. "Is she back?"

"*Nee*, Maddie hasn't had the need for her imaginary friend since Willis and Eva married."

"And now she has a little niece to lavish her affection on, too. Well, I won't keep you. I wanted to let you know the visit didn't take place." Frank turned away.

"I appreciate you stopping by." Danny stepped out onto the porch. "Did the social worker mention anything about Albert's attitude?"

Frank stopped at the bottom of the steps and tipped his head to the side. "Funny you should ask. She mentioned that he appeared nervous. It made her suspicious that he wasn't telling the whole truth. A quick home inspection showed the place was untidy and short on food. He claimed his car broke down and he hadn't been able to do any grocery shopping, but he appeared sober, so that's encouraging. I wish he would come to me for help. Our AA program can make a tremendous difference in the lives of people with addictions. All I can do now is pray for him."

"I will, too. Thanks for stopping."

"You're welcome, and I look forward to seeing your Christmas program again."

Danny shut Holly inside, crossed the street and quickly entered his sister's home. The men of the family sat at the kitchen table. Eva stood at the stove where the delicious aroma of chicken and dumplings rose from the pot she was stirring. Jane sat in Eva's rocker in the corner, smiling sweetly with an expression of utter contentment on her face as she held baby Ruth. Only Maddie and Bridget were absent.

Danny took off his coat and hat and hung them up. Otto and Harley scooted over on the bench seat to make room for him. He sat next to Willis but kept his eyes on Jane. "You certainly look better."

"Better than what?" Otto snickered and covered his face with his hands.

Danny bopped the boy lightly on the head. "Smart aleck."

Heat rose to his face; he met Jane's amused gaze. "You look rested."

Still thin, worn down and on edge though. It would take more than a day away from Albert to erase the marks of his unkindness. Thanks to his sister's kindness, Jane would have a chance to recover. "Eva, Willis, I appreciate you doing this."

"You are always welcome to eat with us," Willis said. "Your sister enjoys cooking."

Eva glared at him. "I do not know why you are all gathered around the table. The meal won't be ready for another hour. I still have biscuits to make."

Harley nudged his younger brother. "Because it's Otto's turn to tend the stove in the living room, but he let it go out and now it's cold in there. We're waiting for it to warm up again."

Eva pointed with her spoon. "Which it should be by now."

"Why don't you boys set up the checkerboard? I'll play the winner of the first match," Willis said.

Danny exchanged a speaking glance with Jane. Eva noticed and took the baby from her. "I'll put her down now."

When the others were out of the room, Jane turned to Danny. "What's going on?"

"Frank Pearson stopped by a few minutes ago. The child welfare worker paid Albert a visit today. He told them you and Bridget are visiting family out of state. He scheduled another visit in two weeks."

"What? Why?" Jane's expression showed her shock.

Danny leaned his elbows on the table. "I don't

know, but you don't have to worry that the police are looking for you. They aren't."

"So, it was an empty threat." Jane shook her head slowly as she tried to figure out Albert's motives. "This makes no sense."

Whatever Albert had in mind, it changed little. She remained homeless and penniless, but knowing the police weren't looking to drag her off to jail lifted a thousand-pound weight from her chest.

"What will you do now?" Danny asked.

"I'm not sure. It seems I have a two-week reprieve to figure something out. I need money and a place to live."

Albert would keep looking for them. He always bragged about the easy money Bridget earned him. What would he tell the social worker when she returned, and Bridget still wasn't there?

Until Jane found a way to legally oppose him, she had to keep Bridget safe. Once he had his hands on the child, he wouldn't let Jane near her again.

Danny gazed at her intently. "You have a safe place to stay for now."

She smiled at him. "Thanks to you."

A faint blush crept up his cheeks. "You are the one who had the courage to get Bridget away. I admire you for that."

"It didn't feel courageous. It felt desperate."

"I'm sure it did, but it was a brave act none the less."

"If only I had done it years ago. She suffered so much because I was afraid." And alone. "You can't change the past. What you do from here on out matters."

Eva came in, lifted the lid off the pan on the stove and stirred the contents.

Maddie peeked around the corner of the hallway. "Is it okay if Bridget wears one of my dresses?"

"As long as Eva doesn't mind." Jane glanced at her.

Eva smiled. "I don't see the harm if Bridget wants to play dress-up."

Maddie turned around. "It's okay."

Bridget came running into the room and jumped to a stop in front of Jane. She held out her arms and spun around. "I'm an Amish girl."

She looked sweet and very Amish in an ankle-length deep maroon dress and *eahmal shatzli*, the long white aprons worn by little girls. A white *kapp* completed her outfit. The sleeves were too long and covered her hands. She pushed them up and lifted the hem of her skirt. "My legs aren't even cold because I'm wearing extra warm tights. Don't I look pretty?"

Maddie shook her head. "*Nee*, you look plain."

Bridget's smile faded. "Aren't I pretty, Auntie Jane?"

Jane leaned forward to roll up Bridget's sleeves. "Remember, I told you that being pretty isn't important. Our appearance doesn't matter. It's how we act. You are the sunshine of my heart, and nothing is more beautiful than that."

Bridget grinned and held her arms wide. "I'm plain sunshine."

Jane chuckled. "Exactly."

"Can we go play on the swings for a while?" Maddie asked.

Eva considered the request for a few seconds, then nodded. "If you both put snow pants on and be careful crossing the road. Make sure you hold Bridget's hand, Maddie."

"I will."

Jane pressed her lips together. "Bridget shouldn't go. I don't like to let her out of my sight."

Danny stood. "I'll go with them. She's been stuck inside all day. A little fresh air will do her *goot*."

Jane wanted to argue but realized that he was right. "Okay, but not for long and keep a close eye on her."

He chuckled. "I watch a school full of children for a living every day. I think I can handle two *kinder* for half an hour."

The girls reappeared with snow pants under their dresses. Maddie pulled on her overshoes by the front door. Bridget started to put on her pink boots, but Danny stopped her. Picking up her left one, he bent the toe showing the duct tape had split. "These won't keep your feet dry."

"I don't have any others."

Relieved that Bridget couldn't go out, and she wasn't the one stopping her fun, Jane held out her hand. "I'll fix them tonight and you can go out tomorrow."

"Oh, please, Jane. My feet won't be very cold."

Danny rubbed his chin. "I think if you put your boots on and put them inside Otto's overshoes, they should fit and keep your toes dry. They'll be big on your feet so don't trip when you walk."

It was a suitable solution, but Jane would rather have Bridget stay with her. However, the grin on the child's face kept her from objecting.

After Danny helped Bridget don her adjusted footwear, Maddie put her large black bonnet on Bridget and tied the ribbons under her chin. "Now you look Amish for sure and certain."

Bridget patted the brim. "This is your hat. What will you wear?"

Maddie got another one from a peg. "I'll wear Eva's. She won't mind."

They slipped into their dark woolen coats. "Now we're twins," Bridget declared.

Jane smiled. More like sisters. One a smaller version of the other. Maddie charged out the door with Bridget close behind her.

Danny nodded to Jane. "I'll keep an eye on them. Don't worry."

"Good advice but not easily achieved."

He grinned and followed the girls outside.

Jane went into the living room where one window overlooked the school grounds. Danny was holding the girls by the hand as they crossed the road and trudged through the snow the plow had piled across the school's driveway. A car she recognized pulled up behind him and stopped. Panic choked her.

Alfred.

Jane pressed her hands to her mouth to hold back a scream.

Chapter Seven

❧

Danny heard a car stop behind him and looked over his shoulder. Stunned, he watched Jane's uncle roll down the window of an older brown sedan. "Hey, you!"

Bridget's grip on Danny's hand tightened. "It's him," she whispered, pressing against his leg.

Thankfully, the large bonnet hid her face. Danny squeezed her hand to reassure her. "You girls go to the swings and wait for me there."

"Okay." Maddie took Bridget's hand and helped her as she struggled through the snow in her oversize boots. They didn't look back.

Danny walked to the car and leaned down to the window, hoping to block Albert's view of the girls. "Can I help you?"

"I'm looking for a woman with a little girl."

"There are only me and the *kinder* here. School is out for the day."

Albert's eyes narrowed. "Aren't you the fellow with my dog?"

Danny gave an abrupt nod. "I tried to return it. You claimed you didn't want it and ordered me off your property. I'll be happy to get her if you've changed your mind. She's at my house." He gestured toward his home.

"I don't want the dog. I need to find the woman who gave the mutt to you."

Danny stuffed his hands in his coat pockets. "I'm afraid I can't help with that."

Alfred's eyes narrowed. "Can't or won't?"

Antagonizing him was the last thing Danny wanted. "Are you talking about the woman and girl I saw at your farm? If I see them, I'll let them know you're looking for them."

"They're missing."

"Missing?" Danny straightened and scanned the area. "For how long?"

"A few hours."

Why was Albert lying? "Where were they last seen?"

"My place."

"That must be three miles from here. Were they on foot?"

Willis came out of the house, crossed the road and joined Danny by the car. "Is something wrong?"

"This man is searching for a missing woman and child."

"*Englisch* or Amish? Who are they? What do they look like?"

Albert's annoyance showed on his face. "They aren't Amish. The woman is young, skinny, plain with brown hair. The kid is little. Three or four. She's wearing bright pink boots."

Danny hunched his shoulders to contain his anger. The man was Bridget's guardian and didn't know how old she was.

Willis leaned down to look in the car window, adding his broad shoulders to help screen the man's view of the girls. "I saw a child wearing pink boots a few days ago heading into the woods. Wasn't that the day your dog showed up, Danny?"

"*Ja.*"

Willis straightened. "It'll be dark soon. Have you notified the police? I can call them from our phone booth if you don't have a cell phone. What are their names?"

Albert scowled. "I didn't say I want the police. I asked if you'd seen them." He tore a piece of paper from a fast-food bag on the front seat, scrawled on it, then thrust the scrap at Danny. "Here's my number. Call me if you see them and leave a message."

Danny took the number. "We'll be on the

lookout for them, but are you sure you don't want to notify the authorities? These woods can be dangerous at night and the forecast is calling for snow."

"No cops." Albert rolled up his window. His tires spun on the snow-covered road as he sped away.

Danny and Willis turned away from the spray of snow Albert's car threw up.

Willis brushed off his coat. "He doesn't seem to be a pleasant fellow."

"He's not. You startled me when you admitted seeing Bridget."

"I find it's better to tell the truth." Willis chuckled. "Just not all of it in a situation like this. Now he believes we'll be looking for a child in pink boots. We'll have to get Bridget a new pair in a plain color soon. I'll go into town tomorrow."

The moment Albert's car vanished around the curve in the road, Jane bolted out the door and ran toward the men. She didn't even put on a coat. Panic kept her from feeling the cold.

She stumbled to Danny standing at the edge of the snow-covered roadway. "Did he see her? Does he know we're here? I need to get Bridget."

Danny caught her arm before she could hurry past him. "I'll get her. Go back in the house."

His stern voice pierced the fog of fear surrounding Jane. "What if he comes back?"

"He didn't recognize her. If he returns, he'll see an Amish fellow pushing his little girls on the swings, but he will recognize you if you're out here."

Danny made sense, but she wanted Bridget in her arms.

Willis took her elbow. "Keep watch from the window."

"Go on." Danny nodded toward the house. "Before you catch your death."

She hesitated but finally walked to the house with Willis. Inside, she went directly to the window.

Danny crossed the snow-covered schoolyard to where the girls were sitting in their swings, moving listlessly. Bridget wore a worried expression. Danny got behind her and gave her a gentle push.

Jane kept an eye on the road while the girls and Danny stayed at the swing set. Albert drove past ten minutes later without stopping. He barely glanced at Danny and the girls.

Danny stopped pushing Bridget then and lifted her out of the swing. They walked toward the house. Jane wanted to dash out, grab Bridget and hide somewhere.

Eva came to stand behind her. "Don't add to her fright. Be calm. Reassure her she's safe."

"I'll try." Sharing her fears with Bridget wouldn't help either of them. Jane pasted a smile on her face and went to meet her at the door. She wouldn't mention Albert unless Bridget did.

"Did you have fun?" She kneeled to help the child take off her coat and boots.

"Yup. Did you see how high Danny pushed me? I almost touched the sky."

"I saw." Jane gave him a grateful look.

He smiled and hung up his coat.

Bridget pulled off her bonnet. "Maddie can make the swing go higher all by herself. She's going to teach me how to do that."

"That is kind of her."

"It's easy once you get the hang of it." Maddie pulled off her boots and placed them neatly beside Danny's.

Bridget's smile faded. "Uncle Albert came by."

Jane nodded. "I saw him."

"Will he come back?"

Danny placed a comforting hand on Bridget's head. "I don't think so. He is seeking a little *Englisch* child. He isn't looking for an Amish girl and you appeared mighty Amish in your bonnet."

Bridget didn't look convinced.

"Did I ever tell you I used to be Amish?" Jane wanted to distract her.

Bridget looked surprised and shook her head. "No."

"Well, I was. I wore clothes like the ones Eva wears and even a big bonnet when I went out." She looked at Danny and Eva as a new thought occurred to her. "Wearing Amish clothing would be a good way to disguise us."

Eva and Willis exchanged speaking looks. Eva sat beside Jane as her eyes filled with compassion. "We would gladly welcome you back to our faith but dressing Amish as a disguise would not be acceptable to us. The true meaning of being Amish isn't in our plain dress or the horse and buggy, but they are important symbols of our faith. Do you understand?"

Jane hid her disappointment. "I do."

Eva sighed. "*Goot*. Were you baptized?"

"I completed my baptismal classes, but my parents died in a car and buggy crash before I took my vows. You don't have to worry that I was shunned for jumping the fence."

Should she share that her parents had already left the church because of a disagreement with their bishop before the accident? It didn't seem to matter now, but it had been the reason she didn't believe she'd be welcome there.

"We encourage you to consider embracing

our faith once more," Willis added. "The Lord guided you to us. Perhaps this is the path he has in mind for you both."

Jane's parents and Lois had turned their backs on the Amish way of life. Would Lois want it for Bridget?

Jane had fond childhood memories of living Amish, but that wasn't reason enough to return. The trials of her life had chipped away her faith in God's goodness and mercy leaving her angry and alone.

Eva got to her feet. "You don't have to decide anything tonight. Pray about it. In the meantime, supper is ready. Danny, you'll stay and eat with us, won't you?"

"Sure. You know I hate cooking for myself."

Bridget leaned against Jane's knee and looked hopefully at Eva. "Can we stay for supper, too? It sure smells good."

Eva chuckled. "Of course you can. You're our guests. I made peach cobbler especially for you."

"I like peaches." Bridget leaned close to Jane. "I'll be good. I promise," she whispered.

Jane smiled at her. "You always are."

As the family gathered around the table, Jane took her place opposite Danny. The way his eyes lingered on her face made her cheeks grow warm. She lowered her gaze. What did he see when he stared at her like that? Glancing up briefly, she caught a smile he flashed her way. He had a nice face and lovely dark eyes that often saw too much. She focused on her plate after that.

Like the Amish families she had grown up with, the men and boys sat on one side while the women and girls sat on the other. Eva placed a steaming bowl of chicken and dumpling in front of Willis at the head of the table. Several side dishes were spread down the center. A plate piled high with biscuits sat in front of Bridget and Jane.

The family clasped their hands and bowed their heads to begin the silent prayer before meals. Bridget glanced around and then looked at Jane. "Why aren't they eating?" she whispered.

"Because they are saying their prayers first," she whispered back.

"The Amish sure have a lot of food, don't they?" The awe in the child's voice brought grins to the faces of the others. Willis looked up and cleared his throat, signaling the end of the prayers.

Eva pulled the bowl of chicken and dumpling toward her and ladled a large spoonful onto Bridget's plate. "Be careful—it's hot."

Jane added a helping of cooked carrots and peas.

Bridget glanced warily at Eva. "May I have a biscuit, too?"

Eva smiled at her. "You can have anything you want, dear."

Bridget stared at the plate but didn't reach for it.

Danny picked up a biscuit and split it in two. "Do you want butter or jelly on it?"

Bridget's eyes grew round. She licked her lips. "Both."

Danny fixed it for her and handed it across the table. Bridget took it, stared at it for a moment, then looked at Jane. "Are we in heaven?"

Maddie giggled. "Nope. You're in New Covenant, Maine."

Bridget took a big bite and grinned with strawberry jam smeared across her lips. "I sure like New Covenant."

She clasped the biscuit to her chest and swung back and forth happily until her elbow caught her glass of milk and knocked it over.

Her eyes flew open, filled with a stricken expression. "I'm sorry. Please don't punish Jane, too."

Willis leaned forward and mopped up the spill with his napkin. "It was an accident, Bridget. Nothing to get upset about. Finish your supper."

"I'll get you another glass," Eva said.

Bridget laid her half-eaten biscuit on her plate and stared at it, her face pale and her bottom lip quivering.

"It's okay," Jane whispered.

"I knock over my glass all the time," Harley said.

"Because you're always trying to reach the last morsel of food," Otto added, grinning at his older brother.

Maddie slipped her arm around Bridget. "We don't get punished for accidents. In fact, we don't get punished much at all."

"Speak for yourself," Otto said. "I had to work off the cost of the window I broke at the school."

"That was two years ago," Eva said as she placed a second glass beside Bridget. "Now, let's get on with our supper. You must eat more, Bridget. You are much too thin."

Bridget looked at Jane. "But I need to be punished, don't I?"

"You do," Danny said.

Jane flashed him an angry glare.

The corner of his mouth twitched as he tried not to smile. "As punishment, you must eat everything on your plate before you can leave the table."

"Okay," she said weakly and picked up her fork. After several tentative bites, she began eating with gusto, and Jane relaxed.

Danny grinned as he pointed to her plate. "The same goes for you, Jane."

Jane smiled back as the heat crept up her face. He was far too attractive when he smiled at her that way. With the severity of her problems, developing a crush on the teacher was the last thing she should think about.

Later that evening, when Jane was helping Bridget get ready for bed, she found the girl had tucked two biscuits into the pockets of her apron. Jane placed them on the bedside table. Bridget watched her closely. "Did I do wrong? It wasn't stealing. Eva said I could have anything I want."

Jane had done the same thing when she stuffed crackers in a napkin under Danny's sofa. They were inside a spare pair of socks Eva had given her. Jane understood Bridget's need to hoard food. "You did nothing wrong. I'll keep those for later in a safe place."

Jane pulled back the covers of the bed Bridget would share with Maddie. Eva had set up a cot for Jane in the same room.

"Can we stay here a long time?" Bridget asked hopefully as she crawled beneath the covers.

"I wish we could, but we should move farther away from Uncle Albert."

"Maybe he'll stop looking for us."

That would be nice, but Jane didn't hold out much hope.

Bridget wiggled farther under the covers. "Maddie says I should ask God to do that when I say my prayers. He let me see Holly again, so I know he listens."

Jane wasn't so sure. The puppy had triggered the dilemma she found herself in.

Bridget yawned. "Tell me a story from my momma's book, Auntie Jane."

Jane sighed heavily. "I can tell you a story, but you will have to close your eyes and remember the drawings your mother made. Uncle Albert wouldn't let me bring her book."

Bridget frowned. "But I need to see her pictures. She drew them for me."

"I know and I'm sorry."

"You should have brought it with us. I want my momma's pictures." Tears filled her eyes.

"Remember the one with the little angel who came down on Christmas? You haven't forgotten the face of that beautiful child. Close your eyes and see it now. In the middle of a chilly winter night, a special angel came down from heaven and landed in my arms." It was the story of Bridget's birth on a snowy Christmas night. Lois had captured her newborn baby's face perfectly.

"I can't see it." Bridget started sobbing. She turned on her side and buried her face in her pillow.

Jane wanted to do the same. She laid her hand on Bridget's shoulder. "You're tired and upset, but it will all be okay."

Bridget shrugged off her touch. "No, it won't."

Maddie came into the room. "Bridget, what's wrong?"

"Jane left my book behind."

"You can have one of my books."

"It's my special one. Momma made it for me."

It was clear Maddie didn't understand, but that didn't hinder her sympathy. She crawled into bed with Bridget and slipped her arms around the younger child. "That must make you very sad. I'm sorry."

It was hard to watch someone else comforting Bridget. Jane was the only person the child had to turn to in the past. Suddenly, it was clear how much Jane needed Bridget's comfort, too. Being shut out made her feel more alone than ever.

She left the bedroom and walked into the kitchen. Danny stood by the door putting on his coat and hat. "I thought you'd be fast asleep by now."

"Too much rest yesterday. Perhaps a short walk will clear my head." She had to figure out a way to keep Bridget safe and get her away.

Danny cocked his head to the side. "It's freezing outside. Are you sure you want to do that?"

"I'm sure." Maybe it wasn't logical, but she needed to get out.

"I'm going home anyway. I can keep you company if you'd like."

Until this moment, she didn't realize that companionship was exactly what she needed. "If you don't mind."

"Not at all."

He held her coat so she could slip it on. It was a simple gesture but oddly comforting. When he handed her Eva's bonnet, she looked at him in surprise. "I thought using Amish clothing as a disguise wasn't acceptable."

"I'm not trying to hide your identity. I'm trying to keep your head warm. You didn't have a hat when you arrived at my place."

"It's still at Albert's cabin. Along with some other things." She tied the bonnet ribbons under her chin as she fought back tears.

He opened the door. "I sense something important had to be left behind."

"Something I cherish dearly." She walked out into the chilly night air. The sky was crystal clear overhead. Her eyes slowly adjusted to the darkness as a million stars appeared. The forest was a black bulk beyond the snow-covered schoolyard that sparkled in the starlight.

Danny began walking toward the school and Jane fell into step beside him. He didn't pester her with questions. Instead, he provided a quiet, powerful presence that soothed her frayed nerves.

He walked past the school and stopped at the swing set and sat down. "This is my thinking spot."

She sat in the one beside him. "I had one in the hayloft of our barn. Do you spend much time here?"

"Enough."

"And what do you think about?"

He shook his head. "You don't want to know. My life is boring."

She cast a sidelong glance his way. He seemed so at ease, so sure of himself. It must be wonderful to have a job and a home, friends and family who cared. She had almost forgotten what it felt like not living in fear. "Do you like being a teacher?"

Chuckling, he took a step back, picked up his feet and began swinging. "Most days. Other days are a challenge."

"What kinds of problems do you have?"

"You mean other than two runaways arriving on my doorstep in the middle of a snowstorm?"

Embarrassed, she looked away. "I didn't know where else to go."

"I'm glad you came to me. Really. As for my problems, they're the same ones facing other teachers. I have excellent students and poor students. How do I keep the smart ones interested and motivate the slower learners to push themselves? Is there enough money in the budget for new workbooks? Where can I cut expenses? How should I deal with the class clown or a bully? When a child falls behind, can I discover why and help?"

"Where do you find the answers?"

"Eva helps a lot. She taught here a year before I took the job. There's also a monthly publication for Amish teachers called the *Blackboard Bulletin.* Teachers from across the country write about their experiences, share helpful hints and answer questions new teachers ask. And *Gott* supplies me with answers when I turn to Him."

Jane wasn't ready to depend on God again.

Danny dragged his feet to stop his motion and gazed at her. "What are you going to do, Jane?"

"I can't stay here."

"I know."

"I need money, enough to get a bus ticket to take Bridget away from here, but first I have to go back to the cabin." The chill that raced through her had nothing to do with the frigid night air.

"Why?"

"To recover what belongs to me and to Bridget." After all Bridget had endured, she deserved to have the one thing she treasured above all else. Her mother's sketches.

"Are you sure you want to face him? What about Bridget?"

"I won't allow her anywhere near him, but I need to go back. He sometimes takes odd jobs. If I watched the cabin, I could go in when he's gone, but that might take days. I can't keep Bridget out in the cold with me."

"Bridget will be safe with Eva, and my sister won't mind watching her."

Jane could observe the cabin and not worry about her if Eva agreed to keep her. "Maybe I can do that."

"Goot." Danny drew a deep breath. "Jane, I'd like to speak to our bishop about you and Bridget."

She frowned. "Why?"

"Because Bishop Schultz may be the best person to help you decide what to do."

Jane's heart thudded painfully in her chest. "Elmer Schultz, the shed builder?"

Danny grinned. *"Ja,* do you know him?"

Albert didn't like the Amish, but he sometimes did odd jobs for an Amish man named Elmer Schultz. Jane didn't know he was the bishop of these people. Her haven wasn't so safe after all.

"No. You can't tell him we're here." Jumping to her feet, she bolted for the house.

Chapter Eight

Danny didn't see Jane or Bridget for the next four days because Eva insisted they needed time to rest and recuperate and wouldn't let him come in. He reluctantly agreed with his sister's assessment, but he missed her cooking and he missed Jane. She'd become important to him. Maddie stopped at his place after school to collect Holly for an hour each evening, and he got updates from her. Mostly he heard Bridget and Jane were "fine" and nothing else.

On Monday morning, Danny couldn't stand it any longer. He had to see for himself how they were recovering. Making his way to his sister's house with Holly, he rehearsed a story to argue his way in if needed.

Pausing on his sister's front step, he considered skipping breakfast one more day, but he couldn't shake his pressing need to see Jane.

He looked at the puppy beside him. "Okay, I want to see Jane, but only because I need to make sure she's getting better. This has all been my fault."

Danny pointed at the pup. "You be on your best behavior. Eva doesn't like dogs in the house. I figure we'll both get scolded, but hopefully she'll feed me today."

Holly whined, cocked her head to the side and scratched at the door. Danny listened, too. Was someone crying?

He opened the door and stepped into pandemonium.

Jane paced the floor, holding Bridget as the child sobbed her heart out. Willis, Otto and Harley stood grouped at the living room door, looking helpless as Willis tried to comfort screaming baby Ruth. Eva sought to distract Bridget by offering her a doughnut. Maddie waved a doll at her. Jane looked exhausted and ready to collapse. Everyone still wore their night clothes.

Holly barked sharply. Bridget stopped crying and pushed against Jane to let her down. "I want Holly."

Jane lowered her to the floor. Bridget dashed to the puppy and threw her arms around the dog who immediately started licking her face. Bridget's wailing gave way to short, hiccupping sobs.

Eva collapsed onto a kitchen chair. "Perfect timing, little *brudder*."

She held out her arms and Willis quickly gave her Ruth. The baby quieted. Eva got up and went down the hall with her.

Maddie joined Bridget on the floor to pet the ecstatic puppy. Bridget wiped her eyes and sniffled. Jane crossed her arms over her chest and leaned against the wall.

Danny cleared his throat. "Dare I ask what precipitated this meltdown?"

Jane straightened. "She had a bad dream, woke up crying and wanted her book. It's still at the cabin."

"A missing book caused this?" Danny hung up his hat.

Bridget scowled at him. "It's my special book."

He realized he'd made a mistake. "Sorry, I didn't know."

"My sister was a talented artist," Jane said. "She compiled a book of sketches for Bridget to enjoy when she was older. That sketch pad is the only thing we have that belonged to her."

Willis, Harley and Otto moved cautiously into the kitchen and took their seats. Maddie and Bridget stayed on the floor with Holly. Everyone had their attention on the entertaining puppy playing tug-of-war with the belt on Maddie's robe.

Danny tipped his head toward the living room and Jane followed him. They settled on opposite ends of the sofa. Jane crossed her arms tightly around her middle. He struggled to find something to say.

"How have…" they both spoke at once.

"Sorry." Danny held his hand toward her. "You first."

"How have you been?"

"Me? Fine. You?"

"Your sister has been coddling us."

"Goot." He rubbed his sweaty palms on his pant legs.

Jane glanced at him from beneath lowered lashes. "Did I—did I do something to make you angry?"

"Me? Of course not. Why would you think that?"

"You've stayed away."

Danny wished he'd come sooner. "Oh, that. Eva didn't want you to be bothered."

"So you aren't upset with me?"

"Absolutely not."

Jane relaxed. "That's good."

Danny noticed a pungent odor and looked toward the kitchen where black smoke curled above the stove. "Eva, something's burning!"

"Oh, the oatmeal!" Eva dashed in beating Danny to the stove and pulled a pan off the fire.

"I'm sorry Bridget distracted everyone." Jane pressed a hand to her cheek. Danny caught the glint of tears in her eyes.

Willis cast an amused glance at Eva. "It wasn't her fault, Jane. We'll blame Holly's antics this time. I should have noticed, but isn't the first time my dear wife has burned breakfast."

She stuck out her tongue at him. "*Kinder*, would you like your *brudder* to start cooking for you again?"

"*Nee,*" the boys said quickly.

"Please, not that." Maddie made a face.

"I remember the first meal you brought to this house," Otto said. "It was delicious."

Willis grinned at Eva. "That was when the *kinder* decided I should marry you."

"It was Bubble's idea first." Maddie giggled.

Everyone laughed. Jane looked perplexed. "Who is Bubble?"

"Maddie had an imaginary friend when she was younger," Danny explained.

"She got me in lots of trouble. A bear almost ate me."

Bridget's eyes grew wide. "It did?"

"Yup. Sadie Sue saved me."

Bridget hugged Holly and kissed her nose. "You would protect me from a bear, too, wouldn't you?" The dog answered with a barrage of puppy kisses.

Danny tried not to laugh at the image of the scrawny, friendly pup going up against a bear. "Maybe when she's older."

Eva scraped the burned cereal into the trash. "Go get dressed for school while I make more oatmeal."

Maddie got up off the floor. "Can Bridget come to school with us today, Danny?"

"I don't know. Can she?" He looked to Jane.

More relieved than she cared to admit at Danny's return, Jane considered his request. Letting Bridget out of her sight would be hard, but Jane knew Danny hoped she'd allow it. It would be a big step.

The past few days have given her time to get past her initial panic. Rest and plenty of hearty food had allowed Jane to think clearly again. She couldn't keep running without a plan. It had also given her far too much time to think about the disturbing man, Danny Coblentz. He set her on edge in ways she didn't understand.

Danny turned to Bridget. "Would you like to visit our school today?"

She frowned. "Can Holly come?"

He shook his head. "I'm afraid not but you can visit her at lunch."

Looking disappointed she glanced at Jane. "What about Auntie Jane? Can she come?"

Danny smiled. "Of course. What do you say, Jane? Are you ready to go to the head of the class?"

She bit her bottom lip. "I don't know. Word might get back to Albert that she's there."

"You said he doesn't care for Amish folks. Why would he speak to any of us? He hasn't been about. We've all kept a lookout and none of us have seen him."

Willis and Harley agreed.

Bridget clasped her hands together. "Please, Auntie Jane? I want to go."

Still unsure, Jane nodded anyway. "I guess so."

"Yea!" Maddie hopped up and down. "You'll get to meet all my friends. Come get dressed."

Danny smiled at Jane. "Another brave decision."

After breakfast, Jane helped Eva by drying the dishes as Eva washed them, but she couldn't stop thinking about Bridget. She'd been so excited to go to school with Maddie that she hadn't even said goodbye. Jane battled the bleak feeling that Bridget didn't need her as much as she once had. She would soon be more interested in spending time with her friends than with her aunt.

"I think that mug is dry enough." The humor in Eva's voice made Jane blush.

"Sorry." She put the crockery in the cupboard and reached for a plate to dry.

"Danny will make sure Bridget's okay. He's very good with children and they love him."

Jane nodded. "Except for the time she was in foster care, she's rarely been out of my sight."

"Why don't you and I go visit the class later this morning."

Jane glanced at Eva and saw understanding in her eyes. Danny's sister was proving to be a dear, sympathetic friend. "Danny invited me but was he only being kind? Wouldn't we distract the children?"

"*Nee*, mothers drop in all the time. We'll bake some cookies to take as treats."

Relieved to have an excuse to check on Bridget, Jane eagerly agreed. "Wonderful."

Eva gestured toward the plate in Jane's hand. "That one is dry, too."

Jane shared a smile with Eva and they both chuckled.

An hour later, with a small basket full of warm gingersnaps in her hands, Jane followed Eva outside. Jane checked the road and surrounding area for any sign of Albert's car but saw nothing out of the ordinary. Relieved, she crossed the highway and entered the school.

Although she had been in the building before, she hadn't paid attention to the room itself. Tall windows along both walls allowed plenty of light to flood the space. The floor, made up of wide wooden planks, bore the scars of heavy use. The desks themselves were typical of Amish schools, arranged in rows with the wide aisle down the center of the room. Well-used, they were beige metal with attached seats that swiveled. The wooden lids lifted to allow access to books and supplies. Jane remembered scratching the name of a boy she liked inside hers. It seemed like a lifetime ago.

Danny sat behind a desk in front of a blackboard that displayed math problems. A large bookshelf off to one side held dozens of books. Jane wished she could explore the titles to see if there were any old favorites or something new that Bridget might enjoy. Bridget, another girl and a boy sat beside Danny at small student desks. Each one bent over a sheet of paper with crayons in their hands and looks of intense concentration on their faces.

Eva gestured to several folding chairs at the back of the room. "Let's take a seat. They'll have a break for recess in a few minutes."

Bridget looked up and caught sight of Jane. Taking her paper, she walked toward the back of the room.

Danny looked up. "Bridget, come back to your seat."

She paid no heed. "Look what I drew, Auntie Jane."

At a nod from Danny, Maddie caught up with her. "You're not supposed to leave your seat without the teacher's permission, Bridget."

Bridget frowned. "But I want to show Auntie Jane my picture."

"You'll have to wait until class is dismissed for recess."

"What's recess?"

"The best part of school," a boy seated by the aisle said with a grin. "It's when we get to go out and play."

Maddie took Bridget's hand to lead her back, but Bridget pulled away. Although Jane wanted to gather her in a fierce hug and praise her artwork, she refrained. "Go back to your seat, Bridget. I'll be here until recess."

Bridget looked ready to object, but she allowed Maddie to lead her back to her desk.

Jane caught Danny's smile and nod of approval. Surprised by how much it pleased her, she felt her cheeks grow warm.

Twenty minutes later, Danny stood up. "Put your books away. I see my sister and her friend have come to visit. Any chance that basket contains treats, Eva?"

"It does. I made gingersnap cookies for the children to enjoy."

"One of my favorites. All right, you may each take one cookie and then go out for recess. Our guest will go first." He nodded to Bridget.

She got up, hurried to Jane and climbed in her lap. "Want to see my picture?"

"Of course I do, but don't you want a cookie?"

Bridget nodded vigorously and took one from Eva. The other students lined up in an orderly fashion, welcomed Jane to their school, thanked her and Eva for the treats, took their cookies and went to the cloakroom for their coats, mittens and hats.

All the children, except Maddie and Bridget, went outside. Danny strolled over to the two women. "Is there a cookie for the teacher?"

Eva grinned. "I think there's one left."

He settled himself in the folding chair beside Jane. "May I see your picture, too, Bridget?"

She unfolded her drawing and held it up. "It's Holly."

"I see that. I like her long ears. It's very *goot*."

His praise for the stick-figure dog with huge ears warmed Jane's heart. The more she got to know him the better she liked him.

"Can Holly come out for recess, too?" Bridget asked.

Worried that Albert was still looking for them and might spot Bridget if she were outside with the puppy, Jane shook her head. "I don't think that's a good idea. Are you ready to come back to Eva's house with me?"

Bridget slid off Jane's lap. "No, I want to stay at school and have recess."

Jane hid the sting of Bridget's rejection. "All right, but you have to mind your teacher."

"I will."

"Make sure you wear your mittens and your hat," Jane added quickly.

"And my new boots that Willis bought for me. Come on, Maddie." Bridget started for the cloakroom, then turned around and came running back. "Keep my picture safe, Auntie Jane. Don't lose it like my book."

The sudden lump in her throat kept Jane from speaking.

Eva got up. "I should get home so Willis can get back to working at his forge instead of babysitting. Not that he minds. He's a wonderful father. Have the children decided on their Christmas program?"

Danny leaned back in his chair. "They have. We'll sing three songs, recite three Christmas poems, have one skit, and then for our big play, the children have chosen to do a play called, *The Trouble With Newest Angel*. It's in the style of *The Littlest Angel*, by Charles Tazewell."

Eva grinned. "A great story. One of my favorite books at Christmas. The *kinder* will do a *wunderbar* job."

"I hope you're right." He didn't sound certain. "The youngest ones will have the most lines to learn. It's risky. We'll start rehearsing after they come in from recess. Jane, you're welcome to stay and watch."

"No, thank you. I have something I must do. Take care of Bridget until I get back."

"Back from where?"

"I need to get Bridget's book."

He frowned. "You're going back to the cabin today? Is that wise? What if your uncle is there?"

"I must try. It means so much to her."

"Okay. She'll be safe with us until you return."

Trusting Danny and Eva to look after Bridget was something Jane couldn't have imagined barely a week ago. She'd found people to depend on here. Friends. Dear friends.

"Danki." The Amish word slipped out effortlessly.

He noticed because his gaze softened. "Be careful, Jane."

She stood to leave before her courage wavered. "Take care of my girl."

Outside she paused on the steps looking for Bridget. A group of children were busy building a snow fort. Maddie was showing Bridget how to pack the snow to make a wall. Bridget clearly enjoyed the company of other children as she adjusted to life away from Albert. Her overprotective, worry-ridden aunt couldn't say the same. Jane took a deep breath, letting the chilly air fill her lungs and force down her fears.

"Are you okay?" Danny stood at her elbow. The concern in his voice told her he already knew the answer. She wasn't. How did he read her so easily?

Jane gestured toward Bridget. "She doesn't need me the way she used to."

"Of course she does. This is new and exciting, but the newness and the thrill will wear off. Then she'll look for comfort and security where she has always found it. With you. Do you remember how to harness a horse?"

"It's been years, but I think I can manage."

"How about driving one?"

"I had my own pony and cart for many years. Driving is not something you forget how to do when you start at eight-years-old."

"*Goot.* Wait here."

He walked down the steps and approached one of the older girls pushing a little boy on the swings. "Sarah, I'm going to my place for a few minutes. I'm leaving you in charge. If you notice an English fellow driving by in a brown car, take the children inside and have Otto come get me."

She shot him a puzzled look but nodded.

He returned to Jane. "Come with me. The snow is too deep for you to trudge all the way to the cabin. Take my horse and sleigh."

"I don't want to impose."

"I'll be teaching. I won't need for it."

Jane followed him to the small barn at the rear of his property. He slid open the large door, revealing a black buggy and a chocolate-brown sleigh with red runners. There were two horses in box stalls with fresh straw on the floor. A propane heater kept a shared water tank free of ice.

He opened the first stall and led out a black mare. "This is Trixie. She's reliable and hard-working. Brush her for me while I get the harness."

Jane took hold of the mare's halter and stroked the white blaze on her face. The aromas of the barn brought back fond childhood memories. It had been years since she had been around horses, but a welcome sense of familiarity took over. She found a brush and currycomb hanging on the wall, then set about grooming Trixie so no bits of straw or dirt would rub beneath her harness. The mare's sleek, fit condition proved Danny took excellent care of his animals. One more thing Jane liked about him. Not that she needed more. She already liked him a lot. Too much.

When Jane finished, Danny hitched Trixie to the sleigh and led the mare outside. He handed Jane the reins after she got in. "If you aren't back by the time school lets out, I'll come look for you."

His concern touched her as a measure of fear returned. "I'm scared."

"You're as brave as a lion when it comes to Bridget. I have faith in you. Just be careful."

"I'll stick to the back road. If he's there, I'll drive past and try another day."

"*Goot.* I must get back to school."

"Thank you, Danny. You've done so much for us."

He stepped back from the horse. "You'd better hurry."

Jane nodded. "Trixie, walk on." She slapped the lines gently against the horse's rump and the sleigh jerked forward.

The ride through the snow-covered forest would have been breathtakingly beautiful if Jane hadn't been worried about a possible confrontation with Albert. She knew where he kept the spare key. It would only take her a minute to go up to the loft and get Bridget's book if he weren't home.

She glanced at the clear blue sky above the pine trees and uttered her first prayer in a long time. "Please, *Gott*, let him be gone today."

It felt right to use the Amish word for God. Was He listening?

The road hadn't been plowed, but several vehicles had traveled along it. Did that mean Albert was still looking for them?

Jane stopped the horse about a quarter of a mile from the cabin and tied her to the branch of a tree. When she approached the edge of the clearing, she saw Albert's car wasn't in front of the house, but there was a truck parked by the barn with a cattle trailer hooked on behind. As Jane watched, a woman carried two of Albert's squealing piglet into the hauler.

It was Lilly Arnett, the woman who had given Jane and Bridget a ride. What was she doing with Albert's livestock?

Jane kept a wary eye on the house as she approached the barn. Lilly came out leading Mable. The cow balked at the trailer entrance and wouldn't step in.

Jane approached cautiously. "Can I ask what you're doing?"

Lilly turned around in surprise. "Oh! I wasn't expecting anyone to be here. Can you help me get this old gal into my trailer?"

"Why are you taking our cow?"

"Albert sold her to me along with the pigs."

At least the animals wouldn't suffer from his neglect. Jane glanced at the house again. "I didn't know. Where is he?"

"He told me he took a job in another town and wanted to get rid of his livestock."

Jane stared at Lilly in astonishment. "He's gone? He sold the farm?"

"Not the farm, only the animals. Are you a friend or relative?" She tugged on Mable's lead rope.

"I'm his niece."

Lilly stopped pulling. "Is it odd that he left without telling you?"

"I've been away." Was it possible that Albert was truly gone?

"Will you help me load this cow?"

Jane shook off her stupor. "Sure. Her name's Mable. I'll get some feed."

Inside the barn, Jane scraped the last of the grain from the bottom of the feed box into a bucket. She closed the lid and sat on it as Lilly's news sank in. Albert had left the area. She had breathing room.

But for how long?

Chapter Nine

Jane carried the bucket of grain out of the barn. Holding it under Mable's nose, Jane then stepped into the trailer. Mable followed eagerly. Jane left the bucket where the cow could reach it and got out. Lilly closed the swinging door and latched it.

"Now I remember where we met. I gave you and your little girl a lift to the Amish school before the last storm. I didn't realize you were Albert's niece. Not that I know him well. He cleared some land for me last year."

She hesitated, then leaned toward Jane. "I don't like to think ill of anyone, but some of my tools went missing about that time."

Ashamed of her uncle's behavior, Jane bowed her head. "I'm sorry."

"Not your fault," Lilly said brightly. "We can

choose our friends but not our relatives. I appreciate the help."

"Not at all. I'm glad Mable is going to a good home." Jane had worried about her uncle neglecting the animals. "You said Albert had a new job. Do you know where?"

"He didn't say. Seemed in a hurry. Honestly, I got the animals dirt cheap."

That wasn't like Albert. If he hadn't sold the cabin that meant he'd be back. "I wish I knew when to expect him."

"Sorry I can't help. Thanks again. Can I give you a lift somewhere?"

"No, a friend loaned me his sleigh."

Lilly arched one eyebrow. Jane realized how odd that sounded coming from someone who wasn't Amish. "I'm staying with some Amish friends."

"Wonderful people the Amish. We're blessed that they settled here. We're mostly potato farmers in this area, but like far too many rural communities, the young people have moved away. Commercial farming conglomerates are trying to buy up the land. When the Amish came with their horses to farm the way our grandparents did, folks really liked that. They've turned out to be good, hardworking neighbors."

Jane's uncle had such a poor opinion of the

Amish she had wondered if others did, too. Thankfully, that wasn't the case.

"Well, I should get going." Lilly walked to the cab of the truck, but looked back. "You might ask Lou Meriwether at the general store if he knows where Albert is working. He has a bulletin board where people post job wanted notices and such."

If Albert had found a job outside the area, he might have learned of it there. She'd only been to the store twice in the years she had lived with Albert because he didn't like her going out. As soon as she finished here, she'd go to the store and find out what she could about her uncle.

After Lilly drove away, Jane took the spare key from Albert's hiding place under the cushion on the rocking chair on the porch and unlocked the door. The house sat eerily silent. A shiver ran across her skin. She'd never felt welcome here, never felt safe, always worried she or Bridget would trigger Albert's anger.

A quick glance around showed he hadn't taken any of his belongings other than his clothes. The message light was blinking on the answering machine. She hesitated but then pressed the button.

"This message is for Albert Newcomb. Since you weren't at home when I came by, I insist you call our office and schedule a meeting as soon as possible. If you don't, I'll have no choice but to involve the police. We take the welfare of children very seriously. You need to call me." The line went dead.

Was that the reason Albert had skipped town? Jane didn't erase the message but left the light blinking. She hurried upstairs, bundled her clothing and Bridget's into a pillowcase and clutched her sister's sketchbook against her chest with intense relief. Bridget would have her beloved book tonight. Maybe she wouldn't suffer another nightmare. Jane removed her carefully hoarded money from her hiding place and went downstairs.

Albert wasn't looking for them right now, but he'd be back. She didn't want him to know she had returned to the house. He would notice their clothes were missing if he bothered to climb the ladder to the loft, but she'd never known him to do so.

Leaving the house, she locked the door and replaced the key. As she walked away, she didn't look back. If she never saw that cabin again, it would be too soon.

Danny crossed to the window that overlooked his home across the schoolyard for the umpteenth time while the children finished their lunches. He couldn't manage a bite.

Was Jane okay? What was Albert capable of doing if he found her? Danny knew the man was verbally abusive, but could he become violent?

He shouldn't have let her go alone.

"We're ready to start." Otto spoke from the front of the room.

Danny turned away from the window. The students gathered in little groups, waiting to learn which parts they'd have in the Christmas play. He had fourteen students. Sarah and Candace, the two eighth grade girls, had written out enough copies so all the *kinder* had one to take home.

He glanced out the window again, then gave his attention to the children. "Candace, why don't you explain what the play is about."

"Okay. This is a story about a new little angel who has a hard time fitting into life in heaven. Newest Angel is never on time for angel classes. He can't keep his gown and wings clean. He gets in disagreements. He broke one of his wings and can't fly, so he's very unhappy. The play has enough parts for everyone."

"Newest Angel doesn't have to be a boy," Sarah said. "We think Hope should play that part."

Danny cringed but held his tongue. Giving the lead to a first grader, even one as adorable as red-headed, freckle-faced Hope Crump spelled pending disaster in his mind.

Hope made a face. "I don't like to get dirty."

Maddie giggled. "I don't mind getting grubby."

"She can be crabby, too," Otto added. The others laughed.

Candace and Sarah exchanged amused glances, but Sarah quickly became serious. "It's only make-believe, Hope. You won't really be dirty. Maddie and Enoch, we'd like you to play Mary and Joseph. Felix, Phillip and Ben will be the wise men."

Danny had a hard time staying silent. The twins, Felix and Phillip Yoder were prone to stirring up trouble. Mild mannered Ben Miller might easily be pulled into one of their pranks on Christmas Eve.

Sarah nodded to the other children. "Matthew and Isaac will be shepherds. The rest of us will be angels."

Annabeth held up her hand. "Can I be a shepherd instead of an angel?"

"Sure." Sarah made a note on her copy, then looked up. "We think Otto should be the head angel."

He looked shocked. "*Nee,* I can't do that. You know how much trouble I have reading."

Danny laid a hand on Otto's shoulder. "I'll help you memorize your lines. You'll do a fine job."

"Do I have to wear a dress?" Otto's doleful expression made Danny smother a grin.

The twins snickered and nudged each other until Danny gave them a hard stare. "Angels, shepherds and wise men all wear robes, not dresses."

Sarah rolled her eyes. "Please take this seriously. Our parents, grandparents and friends are looking forward to our Christmas program. We want to show them our best."

Candace began passing out copies of the play. "Read over these now and be ready to practice tomorrow."

Hope frowned at her copy. "I can't read very well yet."

Sarah dismissed her concern. "Teacher will help you today. Your *mamm* and *daed* can help you at home. Don't worry. It'll be fun. I've written what kind of costume everyone will need on the back of each play so make sure you give them to your mothers."

After that, the three youngest, with Danny's help, chose what songs they would all sing while the middle grade students reviewed poems and chose the ones they wanted to recite. Annabeth offered to compose an original one. Then they read through the play. Danny had to admit it was a cute story. Everyone in the community would enjoy it. If the children could pull it off.

* * *

Jane stopped Trixie in front of the Meriwether general store on the outskirts of New Covenant. The clapboard building had a long front porch loaded with assorted items of merchandise. Sacks of feed, buckets, gardening implements and a collection of wooden rocking chairs lined it. Another horse and sleigh stood out front at the hitching rail.

A bell over the front door chimed when she entered. The owner, a balding man wearing a brown leather apron over his clothing, stood behind the counter talking to an Amish woman. Jane recognized the dog sitting beside her as the yellow Lab mix she'd seen playing with the children and Danny on the school grounds. The dog came trotting over, wagging her tail.

Jane patted her head. "You showed me the right man to take care of Holly. Thank you for that," she said softly.

"Are you sure you can't supply me with Christmas boughs and wreaths this year, Bethany?" Mr. Meriwether asked. "Folks have been asking when you will have some in. No one will mind if you increase the price."

"I hate to disappoint you, but with Eli and now our twins, I don't have the time. I'm sure you can find someone to make them."

"But yours were always so fresh and such

good quality. The smell reminds people of Christmas."

She smiled at him. "My secret is balsam fir branches."

"If you're sure you can't, do you know of anyone who might make them? Will you ask some of the Amish ladies if they're interested? What about your sister Jenny?"

"My sister already has a job, and she helps me with the babies. I'll ask around."

She looked down at her side and noticed her companion was missing. The dog nudged Jane's hand for another pet.

The woman Mr. Meriwether had called Bethany smiled at Jane. "I see Sadie Sue has made a new friend. That's her greatest talent."

Jane returned the woman's friendly smile. "I thought it was saving Maddie Gingrich from a bear."

Bethany laughed. "You must be a friend of Eva if you know that story."

"I am," Jane admitted, not wanting to say more in case her whereabouts got back to Albert somehow.

"I'm Bethany Shetler. Eva is one of my dear friends."

"I'm Jane." She chose not to supply her last name.

Bethany tipped her head slightly. "Are you

visiting for long, or might you be thinking of settling here?"

"No." Jane adamantly shook her head. "I won't be staying."

"How can I help you?" Mr. Meriwether walked around the edge of the counter. Bethany went on with her shopping.

Jane had already planned what she would say. "I'm looking for someone who does odd jobs. Lilly Arnett mentioned Albert Newcomb. Do you have contact information for him?" Jane tried for an offhand tone, as though it weren't desperately important she know where her uncle had gone.

"Surprises me that Lilly would recommend him, but he's down in Bangor until after the first of the year. Jesse Crump is a more dependable fellow. He's Amish, but he gets phone messages. I can give you his number."

Until after the New Year! Relief left Jane giddy. She hadn't expected such good news. An entire month without looking over her shoulder, without living in fear that Albert would snatch Bridget away. Now she needed to earn enough money to leave New Covenant before then. Maybe God was smiling on her after all.

"Do you want the phone numbers?" Mr. Meriwether's question pulled her back to the present.

"No, I'll check back later. Did I hear you have

a bulletin board with job postings? I'm looking for temporary work."

"By the front door. Feel free to put up a notice." He moved away to the back of the store.

Jane went to the board and glanced at the meager offerings for local work. Her euphoria faded.

Bethany came up beside Jane. "Nothing promising? Sorry, I overheard."

"Since I'm not a lumberjack or a dairyman, no, nothing suitable."

"You can always make Christmas decorations and sell them here. Evergreen wreaths do very well. I've made as much as a thousand dollars in the few weeks before Christmas."

That much money would be the answer to her dilemma, but Jane shook her head. "I don't have that skill set either."

Bethany waved aside Jane's objection. "It's easy enough. I can show you how."

Unused to such openness, Jane frowned. "Why?"

"Because you're Eva's friend." Bethany seemed to think that was explanation enough. "Stop by my place tomorrow. Eva can tell you how to get there. Better yet, bring her along. We don't see each other as much as we used to before our babies arrived."

Hope rose in Jane's heart again. Making

wreaths might be the perfect solution. She wouldn't need to leave Bridget all day to go to a job. "I'll do that. Thank you."

Jane left the store and climbed into Danny's sleigh. Picking up the lines, she sat for a moment as the change in her circumstances sank in. The frigid air stung her cheeks, but she didn't mind. The prospect of a month of freedom and the possibility of earning money buoyed her spirits. Only this morning she'd lived in fear with no way to picture a future.

She raised her face to the bright blue sky where high, tattered white clouds drifted along. "If this is your doing, Lord, *danki.*"

She started Trixie for home, eager to tell Danny everything.

Danny's concern for Jane grew as the afternoon wore on. Trixie could have easily covered the distance to the cabin and back by now. What had gone wrong?

As soon as school let out, he'd borrow Willis's sleigh and go after her. Feeling better with a plan, he got through the rest of the day.

When two o'clock finally rolled around, he dismissed class and hurried to get his hat and coat and helped Bridget into hers. Outside, he found Jesse Crump and his wife Gemma had arrived to pick up Hope. Jesse's team of enormous caramel-colored Belgians cleared snow from his Amish neighbors' lanes and the rural roads. He stayed with the horses while Gemma came up to Danny.

"Guess what?" Hope bounced with eagerness. "I get to be an angel in the school play, but I have to be dirty, too, and I'll have a broken wing."

Gemma smiled at her little girl. "That sounds *wunderbar*. I'm not sure how I'm going to make a costume with a broken wing."

"Whatever you come up with will be fine." Danny looked toward his house and sagged with relief as Jane drove up to the barn door.

Hope pulled Bridget forward. "*Mamm*, this is my new friend, Bridget. She's an *Englischer*."

Smiling, Gemma tipped her head in acknowledgment. "Hello, Bridget. Did you like our school?"

It took a moment for Bridget to overcome her shyness. "It was okay, but you can't get out of your seat unless the teacher says so."

Gemma's grin widened. "That's a hard rule to remember, isn't it?"

Bridget nodded solemnly.

Danny suppressed his desire to rush to Jane's side. "I see your mother, Bridget. We should get going."

Gemma stopped him with a hand on his arm.

Her eyes held a hint of worry. "Before you go, Danny. How Hope is doing in her studies? Is she keeping up?"

Hope had been born prematurely, although no one could tell by looking at the bright and energetic child now.

"She is right on track for her age," he assured Gemma.

She relaxed. "*Goot.* Jesse said you'd let us know if you noticed any problems, but I wanted to make sure. Come along, Hope, your *daed* doesn't like to keep the horses waiting in the cold."

"He has big horses," Bridget said in awe. "Aren't you scared of them?"

"*Nee.*" Hope shook her head. "Butternut and Hap are nice *gauls.* I love listening to their harness bells as they plow through the snow. Sometimes, *Daed* lets me help turn the wheel that moves the blade left and right."

Danny chuckled. He suspected Jesse did most of the turning. The blades were made of heavy iron.

Bridget waved as Hope walked away with her mother. "Bye. See you tomorrow."

Danny took Bridget's hand and crossed the snow-covered lawn to his place. "Bridget, why don't you go in and see Holly? You can let her outside." The puppy wouldn't run off if Bridget was with her.

Danny reached the barn as Jane opened the large door. She smiled, looking relieved.

"I'm glad you're here. I'm not comfortable backing the sleigh into your barn."

He foolishly wished a different reason made her glad to see him. "I'll take care of it. How did your mission turn out?"

Her eyes sparkled. "Albert has left town for at least a month, and I've found a way to earn money."

"Were you able to retrieve you sister's book?"

"Yes." She opened her coat and pulled it out. Staring at it for a long moment, she smiled softly. "I can't believe I was brave enough to go back there. I did it because of you." When she looked at Danny, her tender expression made his pulse beat faster.

She was so beautiful. And forbidden to him. A physical ache gripped his heart. "Something tells me you've always been brave."

"Not brave enough."

"So tell me about this job you got."

"I'll explain, but I need to tell Eva, too."

Bridget came out of Danny's house with the puppy at her heels. Jane surprised him by quickly tucking the sketch pad inside her coat. "Aren't you going to give that to Bridget?"

"Later. First, I want to hear all about her day at school."

Bridget picked up a stick and ran to Jane's side. She waved the stick at the puppy trying to snatch it from her. "I made a new friend. Her name is Hope. Her papa has gigantic horses."

Jane smiled. "I saw them. They're big."

"Everyone talked about the Christmas play, but I don't have a part in it. Maddie said it's because I'm not a scholar." She looked up at Danny. "What's a scholar?"

He grinned. "That's what Amish people call the children who attend our schools."

"I attended school today. Doesn't that make me a scholar?"

Jane shook her head. "You visited school today. You aren't enrolled."

"Can I get rolled?"

Jane and Danny shared an amused glance. "I'm afraid not," Jane said. "You aren't Amish, and you aren't old enough."

"But I'm five. I'm as big as Hope."

"Hope is six years old," Danny explained.

Bridget threw her stick and Holly chased after it. "Will I get to be a scholar when I'm six?"

Jane dropped to her knees. "You will start school when you're six, but it won't be here. You and I are going to move to a new place far away from Uncle Albert."

"Are we leaving soon?"

"In a few weeks."

"Not until after Christmas. Because I want to see Hope be in the play." Bridget wrinkled her nose. "She has to get her dress dirty. She doesn't like that."

Jane stood. "I can't promise we'll stay that long."

Bridget looked disappointed, but Holly returned with her stick and distracted her. Maddie ran up to them. "I finished my chores. *Mamm* says I can play with you and Holly."

"Yeah." Giggling, Bridget ran off with the puppy. Maddie chased them.

"I wish you could stay. For the play, I mean." Danny shoved his hands in his coat pockets. The thought of never seeing Jane or Bridget again hurt more than he expected.

Regret filled her eyes. "I can't chance it. Albert is due back after the first of the year. We must be gone before then."

He understood, but it didn't make it any easier. "Let's go see Eva. I want to hear about this job."

Inside Eva's kitchen, the smell of baking cinnamon and apples filled the air. Danny inhaled deeply. "Apple pie?"

"Streusel." Eva opened the oven door and poked the dessert with a fork.

"Even better. I'm going to have canned soup tonight." He peeked at his sister to see if he could get a pity invitation to supper.

"I know how much you love tomato soup with rice," Eva replied sweetly. "Another five minutes on this, I think." She turned to face him. "*Ja*, Danny, you're welcome to eat with us."

He laughed. "I was afraid you'd never ask. Jane has some news."

Watching her animated face as Jane explained the chain of events that led to her meeting Bethany, Danny couldn't help smiling. Things were turning around for her. Perhaps his interference had been for the best and a part of God's plan for her.

After a hearty supper, he stayed until it was time for the children to head to bed. When Bridget came out to show the family the nightgown Jane had made, he followed her and stopped in the doorway of the bedroom. Both girls dived under the quilts. Jane pulled them up to Bridget's chin.

Jane glanced at him and smiled. His heart thudded painfully in his chest. Growing fond of her wasn't right, but he couldn't help himself.

Pulling out the sketchbook, she sat on the side of Bridget's bed. "Would you like a story tonight?"

"Momma's picture book! Oh, Jane, you got

it." The child scrambled to her knees and threw her arms around Jane's neck.

The look on Jane's face told Danny exactly how much she loved her niece. He found it amazingly easy to read her expressions. Barely a week had passed since he caught her tying Holly to his door, but it felt as if he'd known her forever. Emotion swelled his chest and brought the sting of tears to his eyes. Turning away, he wiped his face on his sleeve.

"Careful, Danny," Eva whispered in his ear. "She isn't one of us."

"I know."

It couldn't happen, but Eva's warning didn't matter. He was already falling hard for Jane.

Chapter Ten

Bridget sat at the kitchen table impatiently swinging her legs when Jane emerged from the bedroom. "You slept a long time, Auntie Jane."

Jane couldn't recall seeing the child so happy and eager to start the day. Bridget had blossomed in Eva's household. Already her gaunt face was filling out. Although her cheeks weren't plump yet, they were rosy from the warmth of the kitchen instead of pinched and chapped from the cold of their unheated loft bedroom.

"Because she needed to catch up on her rest." Eva set a plate of cinnamon rolls in the center of the table while cradling Ruth in her other arm. The wonderful aroma of freshly baked bread filled the kitchen.

Feeling refreshed after an uneventful night, Jane sat on the chair next to Bridget. "I won't make a habit of it. I promise."

Willis and the children came in from outside

shaking fresh snow from their hats and coats. Maddie placed a wire basket of eggs on the kitchen counter. "Chores are all done."

Willis took his place at the head of the table. "Something got one of the chickens. Probably a fox, but snow covered the tracks. We fixed the place where he got in."

Eva frowned. "Did he get one of my layers?"

Maddie shook her head. "He took that mean old rooster who pecked my shoes."

Looking relieved, Eva turned back to the stove. "The poor fox will have indigestion already from that old bird."

Otto and Harley sat down. Jane looked toward the door. "Danny is late."

"He's not coming." Harley snagged a roll.

The sharp stab of disappointment surprised Jane. She hadn't realized how much she looked forward to seeing him. "I hope everything's all right?"

"It is." Eva took her seat but avoided looking at Jane, leading her to wonder if she had done something wrong.

Once their silent prayers ended, everyone helped themselves to the ample amounts of food. Jane couldn't get used to such abundance. A glance at Bridget's face told her the child felt the same. Bridget took a single piece of bacon.

"That's not enough to fill up a growing girl."

Willis added a scoop of scrambled eggs to Bridget's plate.

She pushed the dish toward him. "You should save some for later, for when there isn't enough food."

Willis leaned down to look her in the eyes. "Bridget, there will always be plenty of food in this house. My family will never go hungry. If you don't believe me, let Eva take you down to the cellar."

Bridget looked at Eva. "What's in the cellar?"

Eva glanced up. "Let me see. Carrots, potatoes, parsnips, beets, cabbage, green beans."

"Winter squash, sweet potatoes and pumpkins tucked away in crates," Willis added.

Eva smiled at him. "Jars of canned meats, hams, bacon slabs and produce from the orchard."

Bridget's eyes grew round with astonishment. "All that?"

"Yup." Maddie buttered her biscuit. "Gardening takes a lot of work in the summer. Canning all that stuff is a chore, too. I snapped a mountain of beans."

Otto chuckled. "It's worth it when Eva makes her green bean casserole."

Eva stroked Bridget's hair. "We trust in *Gott* to look after us, but we work hard to make sure we have all we need without depending on others. But, if something awful were to happen, say our house burned down, *Gott* forbid it, or Willis got sick, our Amish community would take care of us by sharing all they had."

Willis pushed Bridget's plate back to her. "So you don't have to worry about there not being enough. Eat up or Eva will feel bad that she went to all the trouble to fix this delicious breakfast, and you didn't appreciate it."

Bridget picked up her fork. "Thank you, Eva."

Willis smiled. "A *goot* reminder. *Danki, frau.*"

Bridget looked at Jane. "Can we be Amish?"

Jane shook her head. "I'm afraid not."

"Why?"

Jane hadn't considered it, but why couldn't they return to the community where she grew up and settle among them? Because Lois and Jane's parents had rejected the Amish faith didn't mean Bridget had to remain apart from it. Bridget needed a security and a strong sense of community. She should learn about it and make her own decision when she was older even if Jane couldn't find it in her heart to reenter the faith.

"Becoming Amish takes a big commitment," Willis said. "You must study what it means before you accept baptism."

"And you can't do that until you're sixteen," Maddie added.

"Oh." Bridget looked disappointed.

A plan began forming in Jane's mind. Once she had enough money for bus tickets, she would take Bridget to Upstate New York. It might be possible to change their names and disappear. Knowing Albert wouldn't be returning for a month had lifted a giant weight from Jane's shoulders. She needed to make the best possible use of the time.

When Bridget finished her breakfast, she carried her plate to the sink and came to Jane's side. "Can I please go to school again today?"

"I thought you could spend the day with me. I'm going to learn how to make evergreen wreaths with my new friend Bethany Shetler."

"But Hope needs me to help her learn her part in the play because it's in English. She speaks Pennsylvania Dutch at home, but everyone has to speak English at school. She's not good at it. Please, Jane? I really want to go to school."

Jane didn't know how Danny felt about having Bridget with him for another day. Was that the reason he'd chosen not to eat with them? She couldn't agree until she'd talked to him.

Eva sat down with a cup of coffee. "Why don't you get Holly and bring her over here? I'm sure you'd both enjoy it."

Jane sent her a grateful smile. "Thanks. I'll speak to Danny later. If he says it's not a good idea, Bridget, accept that and don't be upset."

"He wants me there. I know he does."

After Eva's family left for work and school, Jane helped her clear the kitchen. Then she led Bridget across the road to Danny's house. It wasn't locked. Locked doors were a rare thing in an Amish community.

Holly greeted Bridget with happy yips. Jane walked through the place slowly. Traces of Danny's morning lay scattered about. A dirty cereal bowl and coffee cup sat unwashed in the sink. He hadn't tidied his bed. His dirty clothes lay piled on the floor instead of in the basket in the bathroom. The man needed a wife.

What would it be like to be married to him?

He'd treat his wife with respect; Jane knew that. An Amish woman would be blessed if she caught his fancy.

A sharp stab of envy for that unknown woman forced Jane to realize how much she cared for Danny and how futile that growing emotion was. His Amish faith forbade a relationship with an outsider. They could be friends, nothing more.

It would be enough. She'd cherish his friendship all her life. Because she couldn't have anything else.

They collected Holly, then Jane settled Bridget

in Eva's living room with the excited puppy and crossed the snow-covered lawn to the school. Stepping inside, she saw the children lined up across one side of the room with papers in their hands.

Danny sat in a student desk at the back of the room with his hand clapped over his mouth. She hardened her heart against the leap of happiness seeing him caused.

"That's your cue to come in, Hope." One of the older girls beckoned to her.

"I forgot." Hope crossed the floor and stopped beside Otto.

Otto looked at his paper. "Is it my turn, Sarah?"

"*Ja*, Head Angel. It's your turn." Sarah's tone held an edge of annoyance.

Otto looked at Danny. "What's my line?"

"Heaven is a wonderful place." Danny said loudly from the back.

"Right. Why are you unhappy here, Newest Angel?"

Hope stood silent for a full minute. "I forget."

Sarah whirled away in frustration. "I don't think this is going to work."

Danny stood and walked forward. "Everyone, take a break."

The students dispersed into small groups to talk among themselves.

Jane followed Danny to the front of the room. "I don't mean to interrupt."

He began erasing the morning's assignments on the blackboard. "At this moment, interruptions are welcome."

Something in the way he avoided looking at her made her uneasy. "Never mind. It's not important." She turned to leave.

"Wait." He put the eraser down. "Don't run off because I'm out of sorts. What did you need?"

"Bridget's asking to attend school again today. I don't want her to be a bother. It's okay if you'd rather she didn't come."

"Bridget isn't a bother. She can come every day for as long as she wants." He sat in his chair.

Jane clasped her hands tightly together and gathered her nerve. "I missed seeing you at breakfast this morning. Have I upset you?"

He looked shocked. "Of course not. Why would you think such a thing?"

"I could upset my uncle without trying."

Danny moved to stand in front of her. "I'm not him. I got up on the wrong side of the bed, that's all. It has nothing to do with you. I'm worried about this program and if the students can make it work. It's the first time I haven't been in charge since I started teaching. I'm finding it hard to sit on my hands and not say something."

Relief made her grin. "I'm glad it's not me."

His smile slipped as a shadow fell across his eyes. "It's not you. Where is Bridget this morning?"

"I left her at Eva's, playing with Holly. She loves that dog."

"They belong together. Are you on your way to make wreaths so you can afford to leave us?"

It sounded so final and sad when he said it. She didn't want to leave, but she had no choice. She had to keep Bridget safe. The only way to do that was to get her far away from Albert.

Jane pasted a smile on her lips, hoping he didn't notice if it looked strained. "Eva and I are going to Bethany's about noon."

"I know my sister is eager to see Bethany's twins. It's astonishing how many twins we have in our small community. Bethany and Michael have twin girls. Nathan and Masie Weaver have a boy and a girl. The Yoder brothers over by the back door are identical twins. The Fisher brothers, although they're grown men, are triplets."

"Perhaps it's something in the water." Jane pressed her lips together tightly. That sounded foolish.

He chuckled, and she flinched. Was he laughing at her?

"Only Bethany's twins were born in New Covenant, so the water is safe. The others moved here. Our community is growing. It looks like I'll be busy as a teacher for years to come."

Jane relaxed. He wasn't laughing at her. Danny would never do that. Believing in the goodness of others remained a struggle, but Danny made it easier.

Sarah and Candace crossed the room together. "Teacher, we don't think we can do this play without a proper stage," Sarah said.

Danny frowned. "What do you mean?"

Sarah sighed heavily. "The directions say to exit stage left and exit stage right, but we have no exits. Our players will be in full view of everyone."

"We should've thought of that when we chose the play. Is it too late to choose another one?" Candace asked.

Danny looked at them in disbelief. "The mothers have already been told what costumes to make."

Jane looked across to where they were practicing. Her sister had enjoyed visiting a student playhouse. Jane often went with her. Should she offer a suggestion? Taking a quick breath, she decided to try. "My sister attended college in Utica, New York. We went to plays at a student theater. They couldn't afford fancy curtains, so they hung sheets over a rope. What if you put up a clothesline across that part of the room and hung blankets or sheets to screen the actors? You could even slide them open and closed."

The girls and Danny turned to study that part of the room. Danny rubbed his chin. "A clothesline would be simple enough to hang."

Candace's eyes sparkled with renewed enthusiasm. "*Mamm* might let us use a couple of her quilts."

"That would be colorful." Sarah walked across and showed where she wanted the makeshift curtains to hang. "If we went all the way to here, the shepherds and wise men could slip out the back door after we finish singing, then come in the front door during the production."

"That would certainly surprise the audience." Jane grinned at the enthusiastic girls.

"And it won't cost us anything." Danny smiled at Jane. "The school board will be pleased about that. *Goot* idea."

Happiness welled up in Jane. Her suggestion had pleased him. It wasn't much, only a small repayment for all he'd done for her.

Sarah clutched her papers to her chest. "We should run through the play one more time."

Danny shook his head. "There's schoolwork to be done. If we finish early, we'll have another read-through before I dismiss you. Jane, Bridget is welcome to visit our classroom anytime."

Later, with Bridget happily settled at school,

Jane and Eva traveled by buggy to the home of Bethany Shetler. Jane held Ruth during the drive, loving every minute of cuddling the sweet-smelling baby. As they pulled up outside the house, Eva pointed out Michael's watch repair business in the shop attached to their home. Bethany came out to greet them.

Jane handed the baby back to Eva. "Isn't watch repairing an unusual occupation for someone in a remote corner of Maine?"

Bethany nodded. "It is. Michael has clients all over the United States and abroad who send their valuable timepieces to him. We farm, too. My brother Ivan does most of that work. We also have a rental property my grandfather left us, so we're not entirely dependent on Michael's job."

Inside, Michael joined them from his workshop to meet Jane, admire Eva's new daughter and happily present his little girls to the visitors. It was easy to see he was a proud papa. Sadie Sue kept watch over the babies, too, sitting close to whoever held them.

After the twins had been admired and returned to their cribs, Michael took a seat beside his wife. "Will you be staying in New Covenant for long, Jane?"

"Not long but I'm hoping to earn some extra money while I'm here. Bethany has graciously offered to teach me to make Christmas wreaths to sell."

"I have fond memories of helping my wife collect pine boughs." Michael shared a pointed glance with Bethany, who blushed slightly. "Along with her sister and Sadie Sue, of course," he added.

The warm looks they shared told Jane they cared deeply for each other. It must be wonderful to enjoy such a loving marriage. Would she ever know that kind of happiness?

Bethany leaned toward Jane. "Eva tells us you grew up in an Amish home."

"I did." She sensed everyone wanted more of an explanation, but she wasn't ready to share that part of her life.

Bethany recognized that. She smiled and rubbed her hands together. "Okay, let's make a Christmas wreath. Everything we need is on the table. I have frames and materials left over from last year. I'm happy to donate them to you. Once you've sold a few, you'll have enough to buy more. Mr. Meriwether should have what you'll need at a reasonable price."

Jane joined the others at the work area Bethany had set up on the kitchen table. A half hour later, Jane finished construction of her first wreath. She held it up for Bethany to see. "What do you think?"

Bethany wrinkled her nose. "Perhaps a bit more practice."

Jane sighed with disappointment. It was lopsided. "You make it look easy."

"I've had lots of practice. You'll be proficient by the end of the season. Eva, my *mamm* wanted you to know she'll be over on Saturday to help you get ready for the service."

"I'm grateful."

Bethany smiled at Jane. "Will you be attending our service?"

Before Jane could decline, the sound of a crying child outside interrupted them. She recognized Bridget's cries and hurried to the door with Eva close behind her. Danny stood on the stoop with Bridget draped over his shoulder sobbing her heart out.

"What happened? Is she hurt?" Jane immediately reached for her.

Bridget sprang upright, nearly throwing herself out of Danny's hold. "Auntie Jane, I thought you left me."

Bridget latched her arms around Jane's neck in a stranglehold. "Never leave me again."

"But you wanted to go to school today." Jane looked at Danny for an explanation.

"Everything was okay until after lunch. She became tired and wanted to go back to the house. I explained you and Eva weren't there and she could take a nap at the school. That wasn't what she wanted to hear. She became inconsolable, saying you'd left her. I thought it best to bring her to you."

Jane patted Bridget's back, giving Danny a look of deep gratitude. "Thank you."

"What about the other children?" Eva asked.

"Annabeth's mother brought treats for her birthday. She offered to bring Bridget here, but Bridget wasn't having it, so she's staying at the school until I get back."

Jane felt terrible. "I'm sorry Bridget created such a commotion."

He shrugged. "It's okay. It isn't the first time I've had a new student become upset and want their mother. She calls you Auntie Jane, but you're the only mother she has ever known."

Grateful for his understanding, Jane turned to Eva. "I should take her home."

"We don't have a home," Bridget wailed.

Jane rubbed her back to soothe her. "We'll have one soon."

Bridget sniffed and drew back to gaze in Jane's eyes. "Promise?"

"Yes." Jane didn't know how she could keep such a promise, but she would find a way.

Chapter Eleven

Danny saw Jane and Bridget only at breakfast and supper for the next two days. The weather kept Jane from going out to gather evergreen branches. Bridget wouldn't let her out of her sight and didn't come to school. Danny knew they'd been at his place to see Holly because he discovered Jane had scrubbed his floors and dusted the furniture.

He liked finding her homey touches such as a colorful kitchen towel hanging on the oven handle to brighten the room, a pitcher of fresh-squeezed orange juice in his fridge and a plate of cookies on the counter.

She blushed when he thanked her that evening under his sister's watchful eye. He avoided any more personal comments.

On Saturday morning, the weather dawned clear and warmer, perfect for an outing. He carried a spare pair of snowshoes and pulled a red wooden sled the children used at school to Eva's house. With the sled, Jane could take Bridget along while she gathered what she needed. The least he could do was make things easier for her. Eva couldn't object to that.

Holly frolicked alongside Danny, leaping through the fluffy fresh snow, diving headfirst into a drift, emerging with snow caked atop her muzzle. The scrawny puppy was filling out and bursting with energy.

Pulling out his handkerchief, he brushed off the worst of the snow when they reached Eva's porch. "My sister doesn't like having a dog in the house. I'm certain a snow-covered pup will be less welcome. Be on your best behavior and try making friends with her."

Holly wiggled every part of her body as he cleaned her. Leaving the snowshoes standing outside the front door, he went in for breakfast.

As he hung up his coat, Holly made the rounds, greeting everyone as fast as she could, finally reaching Eva's side. Danny's sister stood at the stove making his favorite breakfast sausage. The aromas of the sizzling pork and fresh-baked bread made his stomach growl.

Holly sat and gazed at Eva with mournful eyes. To Danny's astonishment, Eva bent down and gave the dog a piece of sausage and a pat on the head.

She straightened and caught Danny staring at her. "What?"

"I thought you didn't like a dog in the house."

"I don't. A dog's place is outside." She gazed at the pup with maternal softness. "Only she's much too thin, and the weather is far too cold to leave her out without her mother to take care of her. That is the only reason I'm making an exception."

"And the reason you're feeding her my breakfast?"

Eva didn't even glance his way. "She needs it more than you do."

Holly woofed and licked her chops. Eva gave her a second piece of meat, then stuck her tongue out at Danny.

Jane came down the hall tying a white headscarf beneath her long brown braid. She wore one of Eva's gray work dresses and matching apron. Except for the braid, she could have passed for any Amish woman. She smiled when she caught sight of him. His heart stumbled before racing ahead. No matter how often he told himself she was out of his reach, his heart wouldn't listen.

He pushed down his longing and tried for a casual tone. "You look very plain today."

Blushing, she smoothed the front of her apron. "I washed my clothes last evening. They froze solid on the clothesline. They're thawing by the stove in Maddie's room. Eva loaned me one of her dresses until then."

Holly scampered over to fawn at Jane's feet. She crouched to ruffle the puppy's ears. "You're looking bright this morning. I hope Danny is treating you well."

"She's eating me out of house and home, but at least she doesn't have to go out twice a night anymore."

"Holly, come here," Bridget called from the bedroom.

The puppy took off, scrambling with her feet slipping on the linoleum floor as she dashed down the hall making everyone laugh.

That spontaneous, lighthearted sound and the smile on Jane's pretty face convinced Danny it didn't matter if he suffered a heartache when she left. Seeing her happy while she was here was worth it.

After breakfast, the family gathered in the living room, waiting for their friends and neighbors to arrive.

"Are you going to collect materials to construct your wreaths today?" Eva asked Jane.

She nodded. "I hope to gather enough to work on them all week."

"Who is going with you?" Danny looked around the room.

"None of us." Willis glanced at his brothers.

"We're getting ready to host church services here tomorrow. There's a lot to do. Folks will be here soon."

Jane frowned. "I don't need help to collect tree branches."

Danny didn't want her going out alone. "I'm free this morning. Extra hands make light work of every chore. I know my way around these woods. I also brought a sled you can use to take Bridget along and carry your clippings."

Danny hoped his offer sounded offhand and not like he was angling to spend time with her. He caught Eva's warning glance, but she didn't say anything.

Jane gave him a shy smile. "If you don't mind."

"Of course not. You'll need snowshoes if you're going off the roads and paths."

She shook her head. "I don't have a pair."

Feeling pleased with himself, he leaned back in his chair. "I thought that might be the case. I brought an extra pair with me. Do you know how to walk in snowshoes?"

She arched one eyebrow. "I've lived in a remote cabin in Maine for the last five years. Yes, I know how to walk in them."

"That's a shame. I was looking forward to watching you struggle to get the hang of it."

The sparkle in her eyes said she knew he was

kidding. "Shall we have a race to see who waddles over the snow the best?"

Her sense of humor had blossomed now that she wasn't plagued by fear. He liked seeing her confidence grow. "Nope. I get around, but I'm not proficient."

"We expected you to help Willis and the boys clean up." Danny caught the hint of displeasure in Eva's voice.

He understood her concern and wanted to reassure her that he and Jane were only friends. "It won't take us long. I'll work twice as hard when I return. We can't have Jane getting lost, can we?"

Eva didn't look mollified. "Of course not."

Jane turned to Bridget. "We're going to collect things to make wreaths to sell, so we'll have enough money to get our own home. Do you want to come with me today or do you want to stay here? You can ride on the sled."

Bridget wrinkled her nose. "I'll stay here. Maddie and I are going to clean her room."

Jane leaned forward to look into her eyes. "You understand I'm not leaving you. I'm going for a walk in the woods."

Bridget glanced at the ceiling and sighed. "I acted like a baby the other day, but I'm fine now, Auntie Jane."

"You weren't a baby," Danny said quickly.

"You were upset when you couldn't find your aunt."

Bridget nodded. "I got scared, but I know she won't leave me."

"It's okay to admit when something scares you. You can tell any of us if it happens again." He glanced at Jane and saw warmth fill her eyes. Bridget was the center of her universe. For any man, the way to her heart would be through the child.

Not that he was looking to endear himself to her. Her friendship was all he hoped for. There couldn't be anything else. She might look plain in his sister's clothing, but she wasn't. Nor did she intend to stay in New Covenant. And he was helping her leave.

He got to his feet. "The sooner we get going, the sooner we'll get back."

Outside, he waited on the porch while Jane changed. When she came out in her jeans, overcoat and red knitted cap, they served as a pointed reminder that she wasn't Amish.

A furrow formed between her brows as she studied the snowshoes. "These aren't the kind I've used before. Albert's had wooden hoops crisscrossed with rawhide straps. They're wider than these."

"Few people use the old-fashioned kind any-more. The modern ones are lighter and smaller, but they work better." He held out a set of poles. "These will aid your balance until you get the hang of them."

He helped her strap on the snowshoes and watched her walk about. Satisfied that she could manage them properly, he led the way into the woods beyond the school. "What's first on your list?"

"I need plenty of balsam fir because it has a wonderful scent. I'm to mix them with pine boughs and cedar branches."

"Then we should go this way." Danny led her through the woods until they came out by an alpine cabin on the side of a hill.

Jane stopped to stare. "What a pretty house."

"Bethany and Michael own it. Her grandfather built it when he started the settlement here. Michael lived there when he first came to New Covenant." Danny pointed up the hill. "There's a grove of fir trees about three hundred yards beyond the cabin."

As they tramped on, Danny watched Jane closely. She wasn't as strong as she liked to pretend, but he didn't want to undermine her growing confidence by insisting they stay closer to home. When they reached their destination, Jane's heavy breathing worried him. Leaning on her poles, she glanced around. The trees were all the same size and evenly spaced. "Someone planted these. Should we be here?"

He'd let her catch her breath by telling her the story. "Frank Pearson owns this section of forest. He had it replanted after a fire he caused years ago while camping with some at-risk kids. No one was hurt, but he felt terrible. He wants people to enjoy the woods. Folks are free to use what they like. He only asks that if someone takes an entire tree, they replant one to replace it."

Jane drew a deep breath and stood up straight. "I certainly don't need a whole tree."

She brought out the clippers from her coat pockets and gave a pair to Danny. Relieved that she appeared recovered, he took them and began cutting limbs, filling the sled with piles of the wonderfully pungent branches. He stopped when he judged they had enough material for several dozen wreaths.

"I think that's good."

Jane studied their haul and nodded. "Now we need cedar branches, pine cones and holly berries. Only, how are we going to find pine cones under all this snow?"

"My students have a collection at the school. You're welcome to them. For cedar and holly berries, we need to go over the hill. Let me secure this first." Danny cinched down the load with a length of rope.

Jane stepped away to admire the view spread out before them. He suspected she needed time to rest so he didn't hurry.

When he finished, Danny moved to stand beside her. Down below, the winding course of the ice-covered river glinted silver in the sun. A black ribbon of highway paralleled the river's course into Fort Craig. In the distance, the Appalachian mountain range provided a magnificent snowy backdrop under the bright blue sky.

Danny covertly studied Jane's face. What was she thinking? Was she planning her escape from the place he loved and called home? It hurt to think of her leaving but wishing she would stay was foolish. No matter how attractive he found her, she had rejected the faith he held dear.

She sighed softly. "The world is full of wondrous beauty, isn't it?"

And she was part of it. If only he could tell her so. "*Ja*, it is."

Something in his voice must have given away his thoughts. Her gaze flew to his face, and her eyes widened. He glanced away.

Jane heard the softness of a caress in Danny's voice. He looked away and picked up the rope to pull the sled before she could read his face. Did he find her attractive? No, that was wishful thinking on her part.

She liked Danny. A lot. At one time, the dream of finding a loving Amish husband, raising babies in her Amish community, enjoying the companionship of people she'd known for years, was all she saw for herself. All she'd wanted out of life. That dream faded with the deaths of her parents and her sister, but Albert snuffed out her last hope.

Meeting Danny, experiencing his kindness and gentle nature, had resurrected that forgotten dream for Jane. She couldn't have that life. At least not here. There was no future for her that included Danny. Not when Albert could appear and snatch Bridget away. They had to leave New Covenant.

It was hard thinking about all she had lost, but she had gained Bridget, and that was more than enough. "We should find some cedar trees."

"Of course." Danny hooked the sled's rope over his shoulder and started up the steep hill. She followed in his footsteps, gaining momentum and confidence until her left snowshoe got stuck in a deep pile of snow and she fell on her face.

Danny quickly returned to her. "Are you hurt?"

"No." Embarrassed and cold, but not hurt.

"You need to bend your knees a little more." The way his eyes crinkled at the corners proved he was struggling not to laugh.

She attempted to raise up on her arms without success in the powdery snow. Rolling to her back, she stared at him silhouetted against the bright blue sky. Amazingly, her embarrassment faded. "I take your point. Can you get me up?"

He pushed his hat back and cupped his chin with one gloved hand. "Let me think about it."

She scooped a handful of snow and threw it at him. It sprayed across his face. She'd never felt so brave in her life. Had she gone too far?

He chuckled and shook his head like a dog. "On second thought, I don't see any way I can help you."

"As Bridget would say, you are a mean man."

He gave a hearty laugh, stepped forward and held out his hand. "Okay, maybe that was mean."

Jane considered slinging another handful of snow at him but thought better of it until she was on her feet. He pulled her up easily. Once upright, she dusted the snow from her clothing. *"Danki."*

"You're slipping back into the Amish language."

He was right, but she ignored his comment. Turning, she headed up the hill and promptly fell again.

Danny squatted beside her. "I can put you on the sled and pull you along. We might get there faster."

She flopped over on her back. "Tell me again why I'm doing this?"

A grin tugged at the corners of his mouth. "To make money."

"Right. This is for Bridget." Jane held out her hand.

He grabbed her, jerked her upright with enough momentum that she toppled forward against his chest. He wrapped his arms around her to hold her steady.

Jane's breath froze. The world narrowed to nothing but this man, the strength of his embrace and the painful thudding of her heart.

He held her easily. Looking into his face, she realized her mouth was only inches from his. The earthy fragrance of his shaving soap lingered on his cheeks, mingling with his own uniquely appealing scent. Warmth surged through her body. His eyes darkened as he gazed intently at her face. What would it be like if he kissed her? A thrill coursed through her at the thought. Was he considering it?

She felt him stiffen and lean back. Of course he wasn't. Danny was a friend. She shouldn't be thinking about kissing her friend. What was wrong with her?

A quick mental shake banished the foolish notion. Calling up the memory of a winter outing with her school friends, she placed her hands flat against his chest and pushed.

He stumbled backward and landed on his backside. The look of surprise on his face was priceless. She covered her mouth with her hands to hide her smile.

"What was that for?" he asked in mock outrage.

She tried to look properly incensed. "For laughing at me."

"I'll know better than to do that again." He held out his hand. She took a firm grip and pulled him up but quickly stepped away.

Determined to maintain a playful attitude and nothing more, she placed her hands on her hips. "Which way to the best cedar trees?"

The faint look of confusion on his face said he wasn't quite sure what to make of her behavior. "Over this ridge and down along the creek."

She swept her hand in front of her. "After you."

When he was several feet ahead, she scooped up a handful of snow, packed it into a ball and threw it, striking the middle of his back. She couldn't run, so she didn't try.

He turned around slowly. "Did you just hit me?"

"I have no idea what you mean."

He raised one eyebrow. "It's going to be like that, is it?"

She trudged past him, expecting the inevitable retaliation. She didn't have to wait long. A snowball struck her shoulder, spraying her neck with icy bits. She looked back. He was already down on one knee packing a second projectile. Jane didn't bother making a ball. She crouched and started flinging handfuls of snow toward him in a steady barrage.

The wind blew the icy cold particles back against her face, but she kept flinging. He gave up making snowballs and began scooping handfuls toward her. Soon they were both laughing in the dazzling miniature blizzard they created. Until she lost her balance and sat abruptly in the snow.

He scooped up a double handful and stood over her, threatening to drop it on her head. She ducked and held up one hand. "I surrender."

Grinning from ear to ear, he tossed the snow aside, dusted off his gloves and extended his hand. "Truce?"

Jane eyed him critically. "For how long?"

"You are not in a position to dictate terms."

Chuckling, she took his hand and allowed him to pull her to her feet. She brushed the snow from the front of his coat. "I don't have time to play. Would you please keep on task? Honestly, you'd think a teacher would have more discipline."

"You're the one who started this."

"So you say." She picked up the sled's rope and had only gone a couple of steps when he took it away. Inclining her head, she gestured for him to precede her.

He gave her a long, hard look and shook his head. "I think it's safer to travel beside you than in front of you."

Jane laughed and started walking. She hadn't enjoyed a morning this much in years.

Danny's smile faded as he walked beside Jane. A companionable silence stretched between them as they trudged along. He glanced at her and saw her cheeks were rosy from the cold and exertion. She was a far cry from the pale, frightened woman who'd tumbled through his door with Bridget in her arms two weeks ago. There was so much he wanted to know about her. It might be a mistake, but he couldn't pass up this chance.

"Where will you go when you leave?"

"My parents had a serious disagreement with the bishop of our community in Upstate New York. They were shunned because of it. Father decided we had to move away. He and mother went to look at a house in the next county. They were killed on their way back to our farm. I blamed our bishop for driving them away. I thought it was his fault. I don't know the details of the disagreement, but my father was a stubborn man."

"Like you?"

That made her smile. "I come by it honestly. Anyway, I plan to go back. My parents had friends I hope will help Bridget and I get a new start."

"What about Albert? Won't he look for you there?"

"Maybe. I hope he won't put out that much effort. He's already in trouble here. I'm sure he'll find a way to wiggle out of it and blame me."

At the top of the hill, she stopped and took in the view. "I like it here. I wish we could stay."

Danny watched at her closely. "Do you truly feel that way?"

"What I feel doesn't matter. I must think of Bridget. Albert sees her as a paycheck. Guaranteed money until she turns eighteen. After that, he'll turn her out in the cold."

Danny tipped his head slightly. "Is that what he did to you?"

She nodded. "I knew Albert would see me as a burden once my support money stopped. I did everything I could to make myself indispensable in the weeks before my eighteenth birthday. On that day, he told me to pack up and get out. I refused to leave Bridget. She was a baby.

I told him I'd do the chores and run the farm and keep his house for nothing. As long as he allowed me to stay with her."

"I understand why you did it then but why not leave when she was older?"

"I tried when I was old enough to become Bridget's guardian, but I needed a place to live and a job. I didn't have those things. Without them I couldn't be considered. So I got a job in Fort Craig at the motel as a maid."

"It didn't work out?"

"I worried about Bridget. I walked back to the cabin on my lunch break and found her alone and crying. I didn't know where Albert was. I wanted to pick her up and run, but before I could do that, he came home with some excuse that he was only gone for a minute. It happened four more times in the next week. I gave up on getting my own place to keep her safe."

"That's what parents do for their children. She might be your niece, but she is the child of your heart."

Her eyes brightened, and she smiled. "I knew you'd understand."

When she looked at him like that, Danny wanted to take her in his arms and kiss her. He took a step closer.

Chapter Twelve

Jane read Danny's intentions in the way he leaned toward her. Her lips parted as her heart pounded with anticipation, then with unbearable insight, she knew it couldn't happen. It wasn't fair to him. He would regret it. She couldn't bear that.

Jane turned away. "I think we're done. We should get back."

Casting a covert glance his way, she saw his shoulders droop. Then he straightened. "You're right."

They were both silent as they walked home. Jane had only one regret. If she had let him kiss her, she could have carried that memory with her for a lifetime.

When they returned to Danny's house, Jane saw several buggies lined up across the street at Eva's home. Willis, with a group of men, was laying bales along the corral fence. The hay would feed the buggy horses while they waited to carry their families home again after the three-hour service. Other men cleared snow from the drive.

Jane sat on the bottom step of Danny's porch. "I've kept you from joining the work party. I'm sorry."

The effort it took to get a home ready to host the bimonthly Sunday prayer service wasn't something she could forget. It not only involved deep cleaning the house, but making sure the barns, outbuildings and grounds were tidy and in good repair. The scope of the work involved meant families were asked to host a service only once a year to avoid an undue burden on them.

Danny helped Jane out of her snowshoes. "They started without me, but I'm sure there's still plenty to do. Your branches can stay here in the barn until you are ready for them."

"*Danki.* I don't know what I would have done without your help."

"It's nothing." He smiled, looking embarrassed by her praise.

Catching his arm before he stepped away, she could barely believe her boldness. "You made the day more fun than I've had in a very long time."

His soft smile made her heart turn over. "If

you want to practice your snowball pitching again, I'll be available anytime."

She tipped her head slightly and grinned. "I think my aim is every bit as good as yours. Maybe better, but you're safe. I might need help to get out of a snowdrift again."

He chuckled. "I had fun, too. Next time, we'll concentrate on getting more holly berries."

Next time? It almost sounded like a promise. Was she foolish to hope they could spend another enjoyable day together? If he wanted to kiss her next time, would she let him?

Jane walked away from Danny's place with her heart in turmoil. Inside Eva's home, she found several women she hadn't met washing and drying all the glassware, while others were dusting and polishing the furniture. The room smelled of bleach, pine cleaner and lemon polish.

Jane hung up her coat and rolled up her sleeves. "Eva, what would you like me to do?"

Eva stopped scrubbing her stove. "You are company. You don't have to work."

"I want to help."

"Very well, but meet my friends first. Jane, this is Mari Fisher, Mary Beth Zook and Becca Lange. Becca is Annabeth's mother."

Embarrassment sent a rush of heat to Jane's face. "Thank you for looking after the children at school when Bridget made such a scene. I'm sorry for her unruly behavior."

Becca waved aside Jane's apology. "It was nothing. We all know how cranky a tired child can get. Well, all of us except Mari who's only been married four months. But she'll know soon enough." Becca leaned toward Mari with a twinkle in her eye. "Am I right?"

Mari blushed beet red. "Not until June, but *ja, Gott* willing."

The women squealed with happiness as they enveloped Mari with hugs.

Eva clasped her hands together. "How *wunderbar*. Talitha must be over the moon with three daughters-in-law expecting. Her matchmaking plan turned out to be a great success."

Mari nodded. "She's happy, and so is my grandmother. I thank *Gott* every day I get to share this new part of my life with her after so many years apart."

Becca slipped her arms around Mari and Mary Beth's shoulders. "We're thankful He brought both of you to our community. *Gott es goot.*"

There were murmurs of agreement all around. Eva took a deep breath. "Enough celebrating. This house won't clean itself."

She tossed a dish towel at Becca. It landed on her head making everyone laugh. After that, they got busy on their tasks but continued to chat and giggle. Clearly the women of this community shared close bonds.

A stab of envy caught Jane by surprise. It would be wonderful to have friends to share her joys and troubles or simply visit as they were doing now, turning the task of cleaning into a fun project. Feeling uncertain and left out, Jane wasn't sure what to do. The others seemed to know what needed to be done without being told.

Eva looked up from polishing the stove. "Jane, why don't you take the cushions outside and beat them? But first, check on Maddie and Bridget. They're supposed to be cleaning their bedroom. The ministers will use it tomorrow to decide their preaching before the service."

Happy to be included, Jane went down the hall and opened the door to the girls' bedroom. The bed and Jane's cot were neatly made with fresh quilts. The girls had polished the wooden bedstead and dresser to a high shine. The dark oak gleamed in the light pouring through the recently cleaned windows.

Both girls were busy washing down the walls. Maddie stood on a chair to reach up to the ceiling with her mop, while Bridget was on her knees by the floorboard. She grinned at Jane. "I'm helping."

"I can see that. You're doing a wonderful job. Good work."

"*Ich shaffe goot.* That means *I work good.* Maddie has been teaching me Deitsh. We have to finish cleaning the house because there's going to be prayer service here tomorrow. I don't know what that is."

Maddie stopped scrubbing. "It's church. There's lots of singing and preaching, then more singing and preaching, and then we have good stuff to eat."

Bridget shook her head in amazement. "You Amish sure like food."

The girls went back to cleaning. Jane closed the door, took two of the cushions from the sofa and carried them into the kitchen. "Eva, where is your rug beater?"

"Hanging on the back porch by the washing machine."

Jane located it and was soon hitting the cushions with a vengeance. After finishing all of them, she noticed the back porch floor needed sweeping. She located the broom and got busy. The door to the kitchen opened and Mari stepped out. "Oh, I was about to do that. I'll get the mop and bucket."

"If she hasn't forgotten what they look like," a man's amused voice said behind Jane.

Turning around, Jane saw a tall Amish man smiling tenderly at Mari.

"Very funny," Mari quipped. "This amusing fellow is my husband, Asher Fisher."

Jane sensed the undercurrent of a shared story that amused them both. "Happy to meet you."

"Same." He nodded to Jane, but his gaze stayed glued to Mari. "You aren't overdoing it, are you?"

"I keep telling you I'm fine, Ash. I'm pregnant, not sick. Go away."

He looked at Jane. "Don't let her do too much. She can be stubborn, so if she misbehaves, come and get me."

Ash left the porch without waiting for Jane's response. Mari sighed. A soft light filled her eyes as she gazed at his retreating figure. "It's amazing to have someone love me as much as that man does."

"What did he mean when he said you might forget what the mop looks like?"

Mari chuckled. "That's a little joke about my having had amnesia."

Shocked, Jane gaped at Mari. "Amnesia? What happened?"

"I was struck by a car when I first arrived here. When I woke in the hospital, I didn't know my name. My recovery was slow. That's why Ash worries about me. Let me go get the mop and bucket. I'll tell you the whole while we clean this porch."

As they worked, Jane heard an abbreviated version of a traumatic time in Mari's life in which mistaken identity, a false engagement, an estranged grandmother and an injured baby fox all played a part in bringing Mari the love of her life. Hearing what Mari had endured prompted Jane to share some of her own story and talk about her uncle's cruelty. By the time they finished cleaning the porch, Jane felt she had found another friend.

"You're very brave to strike out on your own," Mari said as they entered the kitchen. Jane didn't feel brave. She was desperate.

In the kitchen, two older women were dishing coffee cake onto paper plates. One woman glanced up with a friendly smile. "You must be Eva's friend Jane. I'm Dinah. Gemma's mother and Hope's *grossmammi*, I mean grandmother."

"I speak Deitsh, although I'm rusty," Jane admitted.

"Ah, *wunderbar*." Dinah's grin widened. She gestured to the woman beside her. "This is Constance. Jane, I've heard all about your daughter from Hope. They are becoming fast friends."

Jane glanced at the women gathered around the table. After sharing part of her story with Mari, it seemed the right time to share the whole truth before her courage failed. "Bridget is not my daughter. She's my niece. We are hiding from my uncle. He's Bridget's legal guardian, but he's a horrible person who abused us."

Jane gazed at the shocked faces of the surrounding women. Would they believe her?

"That's an understatement," Danny said from the back door and stepped into the kitchen. "He's a cruel man."

Jane nodded and looked at the women listening to her. "I don't want to deceive anyone, but I hope you won't mention that we are staying here. If my uncle discovers us, he'll take Bridget away from me."

The murmured words of sympathy brought tears to Jane's eyes.

"You poor child. May *Gott* protect you both." Dinah enveloped Jane in a matronly hug. Jane melted against her as the weight of years facing fear and mistrust fell from her heart.

Eva whispered something in Constance's ear, and she went outside. She returned a few moments later with a tall, stern-faced Amish man in his early sixties. His salt-and-pepper beard reached the center button on his vest.

Constance patted his arm. "Jane, this is my husband, Elmer Schultz. Our bishop. I want you to tell him what you have told all of us."

Chapter Thirteen

Panic choked Jane. Her heart lodged in her throat. Was she ready to do this? Could she trust this man, or would he betray her to Albert when he returned?

Danny stepped close to her. "Trust requires a leap of faith, Jane. You have the strength to take it. I know you do."

The look in his eyes gave her confidence *"Danki."*

Placing his hat on a peg by the door, the bishop took a seat at the table and gestured to Jane to do the same. "Join us, Danny. I think you've had a hand in this for some time."

His wife dished up a slice of coffee cake and a cup of coffee for each of them, then all the women left the room. Jane picked up her fork but knew she couldn't swallow a bite.

"Take your time." Bishop Schultz lifted his mug and took a drink.

Danny clasped his hands together on the tabletop. "I can explain my part in this."

The bishop put his mug down. "I will hear Jane first."

Danny cast a sympathetic glance her way. She took a deep breath and told the entire story, starting with her childhood in an Amish community, the deaths of her parents, her sister's passing and how she ended up with Albert. The bishop continued eating his cake one small bite at a time and taking the occasional sip of his coffee.

Recounting the physical and emotional abuse she had endured was hard. Talking about his treatment of Bridget even harder. When she recounted the last day, her voice broke. She dropped her gaze. "I know I should've taken her away sooner. I should've done something."

Danny reached across the table and laid his hand on hers. "You did do something. You came to us."

The bishop laid his fork aside and stared at Danny. "And your part in this deception?"

Danny blinked hard. "I didn't consider it a deception. I was helping a woman and child in desperate need."

"By concealing them from the girl's legal guardian. Am I right?"

Jane had to defend Danny. "He was only trying to help us. It was my choice to seek him out."

The bishop leaned back in his chair and laced his fingers together over his chest. "We live in a nation of laws. Because we are Amish, we cannot ignore these laws, but *Gott's* law is the highest of all. A man who abuses a child breaks both *Gott's* law and man's law. This is a case for a judge to rule upon. Jane, you and your niece are free to remain here until a court decides what is to be done. I've had some dealings with your Albert, not happy ones, but I have always given him the benefit of the doubt, as is our way."

Danny scowled at the bishop. "He's not fit to be Bridget's guardian."

"While I might agree with you after hearing Jane's story, it is not for me to decide. Jane, because you are not a member of my congregation, I can only give you the advice of a grandfather. You must seek an attorney to handle this."

"I'm deeply grateful for your counsel, Bishop Schultz, but I have no home and only a temporary job. It's unlikely I'd be granted custody until I have those things. Even if the court decided in my favor, Bridget must go back to Albert until after the hearing. He would not allow me to see her. I can't do that."

The bishop smiled for the first time. "A maternal bond is not easily broken. I respect that. What are your plans?"

"Albert is working in Bangor. He's not expected back until after the first of the year. I'm going to make and sell Christmas greenery at Mr. Meriwether's store. As soon as I have enough money to purchase bus tickets, Bridget and I are going back to the community where I grew up. Although I'm not a member of that Amish church, my parents had friends I believe will take us in."

"Who was the bishop of your Amish church?"

"Nigel Barkman. You should know that following a disagreement with him, my parents were shunned. They died in a buggy and car crash a short time later. I'm hoping Bishop Barkman will allow someone to give us a home."

"I've met Nigel Barkman several times at the bishop's conferences we have each fall, but I don't know him well. I'll write and explain your situation. Let us pray my words encourage him to be generous and merciful. Is it your plan to join the faithful there?"

She glanced at Danny. "Since meeting the people of your district, I realized how much I miss the Amish way of life. Can I vow to be true to the church while hiding from Albert?

"I don't think the two are compatible. Once

Bridget comes of age and is free from him, then I'll search my heart and make that decision."

"If your parents had not been shunned, would you have joined the church?"

The question stunned her. "I imagined no other life. After a few months of *rumspringa*, I chose to complete the preparation classes. I looked forward to baptism. But it was not to be."

"If *Gott* desires you to be part of His Amish family, He will make it happen. Never forget that the blood of Jesus Christ has paid for all our sins. Baptism washes our souls clean. I respect your courage and the love you hold for your niece. Albert will not hear of your whereabouts from me or anyone in our church. I pray you find the solution you need to keep your child safe. Danny, we should finish cleaning the barn."

Bishop Schultz stood, carried his plate to the sink, put on his hat and coat and went out.

Danny smiled at her. "I knew you could make the leap. Anyone who can fling a snowball the way you do has the strength to do great things." He left, too.

Simply telling her story lifted a huge burden from Jane. She took a cleaning breath for the first time in ages. She wanted to run after Danny and share her relief, but the women returned to continue cleaning and swept her up in their friendliness.

* * *

Danny joined Willis and Harley in the blacksmith shop where they were setting up benches and clearing off space on worktables. Following the church service, the youngsters would engage in games outside while the adults gathered to visit. Willis planned to stoke up the forge and give them a warm spot to congregate.

Willis pressed a broom into Danny's hand as soon as he came in. "What was going on in the house?"

"Jane shared everything with the women and with Bishop Schultz."

Willis began washing his worktable using a large pot of soapy water that was keeping hot on the forge coals. "That's *goot* news. She shouldn't keep bad stuff bundled inside. It's not healthy for a person."

Danny knew Willis spoke from personal experience. He'd hidden the fact that he was illiterate for years. That secrecy had nearly cost him Eva's love.

"The bishop told her she needs an attorney to help her resolve Bridget's guardianship. She's flat broke. Attorneys are expensive. I wish I could do more. She doesn't deserve this. Bridget needs to feel safe, to stop worrying about food and being left alone. She's only five, and she's faced such hardship. Jane has done everything she can to protect Bridget at the expense of her own well-being. I don't know that I've ever met someone so brave."

Willis stopped scrubbing and looked at Danny. "Oh wow. You've fallen for her."

Danny kept his head down and swept faster. "That's nonsense."

Willis grasped Danny's arm, forcing him to stop. "Are you in love with Jane?"

Danny couldn't look him in the eye. He cared deeply for Jane, but he wouldn't allow himself to fall in love. "I care for her as a friend. I want to make her life easier."

"How does Jane feel about you?"

Danny turned away from Willis and continued sweeping. "She's grateful."

"Gratitude can turn into affection. It's a short step. Shall I tell you to be careful and guard your heart? While it might be *goot* advice, it's useless. The heart rarely listens to advice, even if it's delivered by a well-meaning friend."

Danny looked at his brother-in-law. "My sister was smart to marry you."

"I don't know about that, but she is the best thing that ever happened to me. Trust *Gott* to bring you the right woman, Danny. Don't settle for less."

Danny cupped his hands over the end of the broomstick and rested his chin on them. "What happens if the right woman isn't one of us?"

Willis heaved a deep sigh. "Then she isn't the right one, Danny."

Willis was right, but Danny didn't know how to convince his heart.

Worshipers started arriving for the prayer service by seven thirty Sunday morning. The lumbering bench wagon arrived shortly afterward, delivered by the Fisher family. While the strapping sons of Zeke Fisher carried in the wooden backless benches, Willis and Otto pushed the movable wall between the living room and the main bedroom open to provide space for the seating to be lined up into two sections. One side for the men and boys, the other for women and girls. The preachers would stand between them.

Outside, Danny and Harley parked the buggies and sleighs and saw to the horses as each family arrived. Jane helped in the kitchen. Bridget, Maddie and the other children played tag or hide-and-seek in the barn. Bishop Schultz's arrival signaled the service would start shortly.

Jane took Bridget into their bedroom after the bishop and his minister finished preparing their sermons. She heard the mournful chanting of the opening song through the closed door. Prepared to wait out the three-hour service,

Jane sat on the edge of her cot with Bridget beside her. Bridget clutched her beloved book, her cheeks rosy from playing outside. Every passing day brought her improving health. Jane had Danny to thank for that. The realization that she had God to thank, too, struck her. She silently gave thanks.

"Tell me the story about the dog in the park." Bridget opened the sketchbook to the amazingly detailed scene. "Are you sure Holly can't stay in here with us?"

"I'm sure."

Jane started a story about a woman and her dog visiting the park while Bridget studied the picture and pointed out all the little birds and animals cleverly hidden in the bushes and trees.

The first hymn ended followed by a period of silence. A short time later, a man's voice started the second hymn. The congregation joined the slow mournful tempo.

Bridget looked at Jane. "Why do they sound so sad when they sing?"

"These are ancient Amish songs, some over eight-hundred-years old. Long ago, Amish people were put in prison for their beliefs. Many of the hymns they sing now were written by those people. This one is called 'Das Loblied,' or 'Hymn of Praise.' It's always the second song at an Amish service."

The slow chanting voices carried Jane back to her childhood, to a time when she believed absolutely in the goodness of God. She hadn't realized how much her soul craved that connection until now.

Bridget laid her head against Jane's side. "What are they saying?"

Jane closed her eyes and tried to translate in words Bridget would understand, knowing it wasn't exactly right. "O Lord Father, we bless your name."

"Is O Lord Father the same as *Gott*?"

Jane smiled and nodded. "That's right."

"I thought so. Maddie prays to him every night and in the morning, too. I talk to him sometimes. What else are they saying?"

Jane closed her eyes again. "Your love and Your goodness we praise, that You, O Lord, have graciously given to us always. You have brought us together, O Lord, to be admonished through Your word. Bestow Your grace on us."

"What's *admonished*?"

"Cautioned or warned that we are doing something wrong, I think. Amish folk gather to praise God and be reminded that they make mistakes, but with God's help, with His grace, we can overcome our failures."

Bridget leaned against Jane's side. "I like this song."

Jane hugged her close. "So do I."

With God's grace, could she overcome the mistakes of her past? Did she believe that? Danny did. Eva and Willis and all the people seated in the other room believed it. They were joined together by that invisible thread.

Years ago she'd made a choice to be one of them, too. Then tragedy struck and tore her away from the community, left her swirling in the wind like a fallen leaf. Feeling abandoned by God, she never found the courage to return to the faith that once meant everything to her. Unlike her imprisoned ancestors facing death, Jane had denied her faith.

Albert disliked the Amish, but she could have defied him and walked to services here. Even brought Bridget along to give the child a sense of community and belonging. Had she done so, she could have been a part of this amazing community and perhaps found sanctuary before now.

God hadn't turned His back on her. She had failed Him.

Closing the sketchbook, Jane laid it aside. "Would you like to go sit with Maddie and Hope?"

"Sure. Can I?"

"It might be boring. The preaching is in Deitsh. You'll have to sit still and be quiet. Can you do that?"

"Like in school? I can."

"You may take your book to look at."

"Okay."

Jane found a scarf to cover her hair and one for Bridget, then she opened the door and walked down the hall to the living room. She took a seat on a bench at the back of the room beside Sarah and Candace, who scooted over to make room for her. Bridget went to sit with Eva and Maddie.

Bishop Schultz stopped preaching in Deitsh and switched to English. "Our Lord God does not promise our lives will be free of pain and grief. What does He tell us? He promises to be with us always until the end of time. We rely on Him for our strength in times of trial for His love never fails us."

Jane listened to the words with an open heart. Looking across the room, she saw Danny watching her with the light of approval shining in his eyes.

Danny couldn't find a chance to talk to Jane until after the meal had been served and the cleaning up finished. From the moment the service ended, the women of the community surrounded Jane. It warmed his heart to see her accepted unconditionally, but he desperately wanted to know if her appearance during the service meant she planned to rejoin the faith. A tentative hope uncurled in him like a baby fern in the spring.

His opportunity finally came when she stepped outside to look for Bridget. Her soft smile when their eyes met sent his heart racing. "She's in the forge with Hope and Maddie. Sarah is keeping an eye on them."

"How did you know I was looking for Bridget?"

"Because she's always the first thing on your mind."

"I reckon that's true. It's been a wonderful day. I've made a decision, Danny. I want to return to the faith and be baptized. Bishop Schultz has agreed to help me review what I learned in my preparation classes all those years ago."

Danny's spirit soared. He took a step closer. "Is this truly what you want?"

She pulled her unbuttoned coat tightly across her chest, her face glowing with peace and happiness. "Sitting on that bench, hearing the hymns that echoed from my childhood, listening to God's word filled my soul with utter contentment. I became part of something greater again. I know this is what God wants for me."

"You will stay in New Covenant?" He held his breath waiting for her answer.

The happiness faded from her eyes. "Bridget

isn't safe here. Albert has the law on his side. If he finds her, I'll lose her."

Danny's newfound hope crumbled, but he couldn't give up. "We can find a way around the law. We'll get an attorney. *Gott* will protect you both and so will I if you stay." He was begging and didn't care that she knew it.

"Danny, I can't."

Looking down, he nodded, knowing he'd lost the woman who had come to mean so much to him. "I understand."

"I'm sorry."

He put on a brave face. "No reason to be sorry. You love her. You want what's best for her. I pray you find happiness and security wherever you go." She would take his heart with her.

"Everything I have gained is due to you. I'll be forever grateful."

"Du bischt wilkumm." He wanted more than her gratitude, but it was all she had to give. She'd found her way back to God, but not to him. Tears stung his eyes. He turned away before she realized how much she'd hurt him.

Chapter Fourteen

Jane's sense of profound peace didn't blind her to the pain in Danny's eyes. Perhaps because of the stillness in her soul, she saw it more clearly. An overwhelming desire to comfort him filled her heart. He cared about her, wanted her to stay and be a part of this wonderful community. She wanted the same thing, but she couldn't. Bridget's safety was more important.

Turning around, she found Eva watching her. "My brother likes you a lot."

"And I like him." It was more than that. Jane was halfway in love with him, but she refused to let those feelings grow.

"I worried when I saw him falling for someone forbidden. Then today I thought perhaps there is hope for the two of you."

Jane did her best not to think of Danny's pain. Bridget came first. "If things were different, maybe."

"I'm sorry it's not to be, but I'm not giving up hope. *Gott* has something wonderful in store for the two of you. I know it."

Jane wanted to believe that, too, but she didn't see how it could happen.

On Monday morning, she helped Eva fix breakfast. Would Danny stay away? She couldn't blame him if he did, but he came through the front door at his usual time. She scanned his face for a hint of his feelings and found the warmth missing from his eyes. He didn't smile. Only when Bridget came in did his expression brighten.

Sitting across from him at breakfast, Jane found it difficult to swallow her food. A covert glance revealed him pushing his eggs around on the plate without eating them.

Would it be like this until she left?

He looked up and caught her staring at him. "I brought your greenery over. It's on the sled outside. Where would you like it?"

She glanced at Willis. "Can I work in the barn?"

"Too cold out there," Danny said before Willis could reply. "You can't bundle branches together wearing mittens."

Eva poured a cup of coffee for Jane. "He's right. You might as well work here at the table."

Danny stood with a grim expression. "I'll bring them in."

"Don't go to any trouble." Jane wanted him to smile, not stare past her with cold eyes.

"No trouble." He went out the door. It slammed behind him.

"Is Danny mad at us?" Maddie asked.

"I don't think so." Bridget put another piece of bacon on her plate. "When Uncle Albert is mad, he yells really loud. Danny didn't yell."

Eva carried the coffeepot to the stove. "Danny has a lot on his mind. We must remember to be kind to him."

The door banged open. He came in with an armload of evergreen branches. "Is this enough to get started, Jane?"

He still didn't look at her. Losing his easy companionship made her want to cry. "More than enough, *danki*."

Eva laid a hand on Otto's shoulder. "Bring the folding card table in here. We'll put it in the corner so Jane has a space to work."

Jane reached to take the bundle from Danny. He moved it away. "I've got it. You'll get sticky pitch on your clothes."

She stood awkwardly beside him, waiting for Otto to finish setting up the table. Eva watched them from across the room with a faint frown creasing her brow.

Finally, Otto had the table ready. Danny plopped his load down. "I'll get the holly berries."

Jane escaped to her room to collect the wire and frames Bethany had given her. When she returned to the kitchen, Eva had a fir clipping to her nose, inhaling deeply. "It smells *wunderbar*. No wonder the *Englisch* bring these trees into their homes at Christmas."

"Let's hope they buy lots of my wreaths." Jane laid her equipment on the small table.

Eva rubbed her face with her hands.

Danny came in with the basket containing the holly berries they had collected. He scowled at his sister. "What's wrong with your face, Eva?"

Jane followed his gaze. Eva's eyes were red and puffy. She knuckled them. "I don't know. They just started itching."

Danny crossed the room to examine her more closely. "It looks like an allergic reaction. The kind *mamm* used to get when she was around fresh alfalfa."

"I've had this happen a few times but never this bad." She pressed the heels of her hands against her face.

"Don't rub it," he scolded.

Jane went to the cupboard and took out a box of baking soda. "I'll make a compress for you."

"Sit down." Danny pulled over a chair for her.

Jane dampened a cloth in baking soda and cold water. "Try this." She placed it over Eva's eyes.

"Is it helping?" Danny asked after a few minutes.

"*Ja.* This is so strange. There's nothing different in the house."

Jane picked up the sprig of balsam Eva had been holding. "Yes, there is. It's the fir branches. Danny, help me take these out to the barn." Jane gathered an armload.

"You can't work out there," Eva said.

"Willis can figure a way to keep me warm. Danny, get the door."

He didn't move. "Eva's right. Take them over to my place."

Jane shook her head. "Your barn isn't any warmer."

"Not the barn. Take them in the house. You can work at my place while I'm at school during the day."

The generosity of his offer brought a lump to Jane's throat. "Are you sure?"

He wagged his head back and forth and then smiled. "I'm sure. You need to earn money quickly and my house sits empty except for Holly. It will work out great."

Seeing the return of his smile raised Jane's spirits more than any money she could make. "I appreciate this."

"That's what friends do."

"Are we friends again?" she whispered, not daring to look at him.

He stepped close and lifted her chin, leaving her no choice but to gaze into his eyes. "We always have been. We always will be."

Jane believed him.

After a challenging day at school in which the Yoder twins locked Ben in the cloakroom while everyone was out at recess and Hope refused to recite her lines for the play because Bridget wasn't there to help her, Danny faced the most difficult task of the day. Going home.

Maybe Jane wouldn't be there. Hopefully, she'd finished and gone back to Eva's house, so he could sit and sulk in peace. He'd done enough of that during his sleepless night as he struggled to accept Jane and Bridget were going out of his life forever.

Giving her the run of his house while he was at school was a small price to pay for seeing her smile. It shouldn't have been a big deal, but knowing she was there while he grappled with grading papers left him feeling like Jesse Crump's Belgians had run him over.

As he stepped out the school door, a gust of wind threatened to tear his hat off. Grasping his brim, he kept his head down until he reached his porch. When he looked up, Bridget and Holly were waiting for him. Holly had an evergreen wreath collar around her neck, while Bridget wore one like a crown on her head.

"Hi, Teacher. Guess what we are?"

Danny fought back a smile. "I think you're a little girl and her puppy playing with Jane's hard work."

Bridget shook her head. "Nope. We're the spirit of Christmas, like in my momma's book. Holly should be a reindeer, but I don't have antlers to put on her head, so she's a Christmas dog. I'm the special Christmas child 'cause Christmas is my birthday."

He had Christmas on his doorstep today, but he wouldn't get to see the spirit of spring, or summer, or fall waiting for him because they would be gone. All he'd have was this memory. "Holly makes a fine Christmas dog, and you are a *wunderbar* Christmas child."

"I think so, too." She popped up. "Did anyone miss me at school?"

"Hope missed you a lot."

"I better go to school tomorrow so she won't miss me again."

He climbed the steps and opened his door. The smell of cooking chicken and pine forests greeted him as he stepped inside. Eva's card table sat in the middle of his living room piled high with evergreen wreaths trimmed with holly berries, rose hips, pine cones and curls of white birch bark. Jane stood at the stove in his kitchen with her back to him.

"Bridget, get ready to go to Eva's house. Danny will be home soon."

"Danny is home already." He walked to the stove, lifted the lid of the pot simmering on the rear burner and breathed in the delicious aroma of chicken and dumplings.

Blushing a bright shade of pink, Jane wiped the table with a damp rag then dried her hands on a towel, looking like a mouse caught in a corner. He didn't want her to be uncomfortable around him.

Forcing aside his depressed spirits, he tried for a jovial tone. "Yum. Smells *goot*. Otto loves chicken and dumplings. I hope you'll leave some here for me."

Her expression of discomfort faded. With his acting skills he should have a part in the play.

"It's all for you. A way to say thanks for letting me work here." She wiped the tabletop again leaving damp streaks on it.

"Jane, that's unnecessary."

"I know, but I wanted to do something nice for you."

He would have settled for one of her smiles. *"Danki."*

She shut off the stovetop and pulled the pan from the burner. "I made enough for a few meals."

"Good. Holly will want her share."

Jane chuckled. Oddly, she didn't seem in a hurry to leave. "How was your day?"

"Not one of my best." Danny slipped out of his coat, hung up his hat and settled at the table. "The twins locked Ben in the coatroom at the start of the morning recess. I didn't discover him until the children returned to class. I should have noticed he wasn't with the others."

Distracted by Jane's rejection, he failed to notice one less child on the school grounds. He hadn't even heard the boy yelling.

"The poor child. Was he upset?"

"Not really. He found the twins' lunch pails and ate their food. They had to go hungry the rest of the day."

Jane snorted and then laughed out loud. Danny's mood soared.

Hearing her laugh made him realize her friendship and happiness were more important than his feelings. Until she left New Covenant, he would cherish the times they had together and stop wishing it could be different.

Jane relaxed. Danny could always make her smile. What was it about him? Yes, he was a friendly, caring man who looked after his sister's family and all the schoolchildren, but what motivated him? What made him into such a special person?

Hoping to understand him better, she dared to probe deeper. "You know my story, Danny. What's yours?"

He glanced at her in surprise. "What do you mean?"

She waved one hand to encompass everything. "Why did you come to Maine? Why are you a teacher? How is it you've never married?" The single most important thing she wanted to know.

Looking uncomfortable, he shifted in his chair and shook his head. "Those are long and boring stories."

She stayed quiet until he glanced at her, then said, "Indulge me."

After a moment, he took a deep breath and leaned back in his chair. "Where to start? I came to Maine at my oldest brother's request, to convince Eva to return home and take care of his sick mother-in-law. His wife didn't feel up to the task, but she rarely felt up to any task. Unkind of me to say, I know."

"Sometimes the truth isn't kind."

"Anyway, Eva had fallen in love with Willis by the time I arrived, and didn't want to go home. I liked it here. So I stayed, too."

The way he finished in a rush told Jane she wasn't hearing the whole story. "What's the real reason?"

He eyed her critically for several long seconds, then nodded. "You're right. I didn't go home because the girl I wanted to marry got engaged to my best friend."

Jane winced at the pain beneath his flippant words. "Ouch."

"Cowardly of me, wasn't it?"

"That's not for me to decide. I haven't always made the bravest decisions. So you stayed in Maine. Why become a teacher?"

A soft smile curved his lips. "Oddly enough, I saw how much Eva enjoyed it. I thought it was something I could try until I found a better position. I worked as her assistant teacher until she married, then I took over the classes. Best decision of my life."

"And no local maidens have caught your fancy since then?"

His eyes narrowed, then he looked down. "Several have caught my fancy, but none have fancied me in return."

"That's hard to believe."

A sharp bark of laughter erupted from him. "Oh, it's true." He drew little circles in the water droplets on the table. "I reckon I'm just not lovable."

Jane glimpsed a flash of pain in his eyes before he turned away. He wasn't angling for a compliment. He believed it.

Shooting to his feet, he grabbed his hat and coat. "The chores won't do themselves."

As he went out the door, Jane moved to the window to watch him trudge through the snow to the barn. How could anyone be more lovable than this amazing man?

All her efforts to harden her heart against her growing affection for him were useless. She was falling in love with Danny Coblentz. Not because he had been her savior, or because she owed him for taking her in. No, it went much deeper.

When she left New Covenant, a large piece of her heart would remain with him.

The next morning, Mr. Meriwether beamed with delight when Jane came into his store with an arm full of evergreen wreaths. "Please tell me these are for sale."

"Bethany Shetler suggested you might let me sell them here."

Picking one up, he scrutinized it, tugging on the sprigs to make sure they were secure. "These are fine quality. I've had customers asking about them for weeks. You're free to set up

a display and sell them to my customers or…"
He paused.

"Or what?" She wondered if this venture was going to fail before it started.

"Or I can buy them from you now and sell them myself. That way you don't have to be here to deal with customers."

A wonderful suggestion. She preferred to stay out of sight, but was it a wise business decision? "What will you give me for them?"

He named a price Bethany had suggested Jane charge. "Can you make money from them if you pay me that much?"

"I'll simply charge a slightly higher price. People will come in for these and buy other items while they're here."

"Or I could charge more and sell them myself."

His smile slipped slightly. "You could, but your time is worth something. If you don't have to be stuck here, you can make more. Last year Mrs. Shetler left her greenery for me to sell. I kept a small commission. I'm willing to do that, too."

"What if you don't sell all I bring?"

"Then it's my loss but I'm sure I can sell them. I know an outlet in Presque Isle that'll take an order for fifteen by Friday if you're willing to do that?"

Jane considered the offer. Half that number were already piled in the corner at Danny's. If Bridget went with him to school every day, making enough wouldn't be a problem except for supplies. "Do you have wreath frames and florist wire?"

"I do. I ordered them thinking Mrs. Shetler would want them. I'm glad I did now."

Jane followed him to a corner at the back of the store where he had stacked several boxes of frames. "I'm afraid I don't have money with me today."

"I'll put it on your account. Pay me from your earnings when the season is over."

She held out her hand. "I accept."

He shook it. "Agreed. How many do you have there?"

"Six."

"Can you bring more tomorrow?"

"Yes."

"Wonderful. Come over to the counter, and I'll get your money."

Jane barely contained her joy. She assumed it would take days to earn anything, but she was getting paid now.

After collecting her money and supplies, Jane followed Mr. Meriwether to the front of the store where he leaned the wreaths against the window display.

"If you were to place one on your front door, people couldn't miss it."

He grinned at her. "Excellent idea. How many more can you bring tomorrow?"

"I'll bring all I have. Do you sell dress material?"

"Only the plain colors the Amish women use."

"That's exactly what I want." She intended to embrace the Amish way of life, including plain clothing, as soon as possible.

After parting with half her money for the cloth, she left with enough material to make herself and Bridget two dresses each and two *kapps*. Resisting the urge to skip down the sidewalk to the sleigh, she breathed a prayer of thanks, eager to share her success with Danny. God was doing wonderful things for her.

The next several days were bittersweet ones for Danny. Each morning he breakfasted with Eva and her family while seated across from Jane, watching her animated face as she shared the latest antics Holly and Bridget got up to as she tried to craft evergreen wreaths. He laughed with the others while hiding his aching heart. Sometimes he thought he glimpsed regret in her eyes, but she always looked away before he could be sure.

Bridget had transformed from a shy, fearful child into someone who rivaled Maddie as the center of attention in the household. Anything Maddie could do, Bridget attempted. She helped with the dishes and the cleaning, gathering eggs, even fed the chickens by herself, trudging out through the deep snow without complaint.

Eva allowed her to help with the cooking and baking, but Bridget's favorite pastime was rocking Ruth and singing to her. Sometimes she told the baby stories while holding her mother's sketchbook where Ruth could see it. Jane must have done the same, sharing memories with Bridget of the mother she never knew.

At Eva's suggestion, Jane made long boughs of greenery for Danny's windows and for the windows at school. Such simple Christmas decorations were the only ones the church found acceptable. Fancy lights and Christmas trees did not suit their plain ways. Each student could bring a candle to set among the boughs, but they wouldn't be lit until the Christmas Eve program. The fragrant scent of pine permeated the school the same way it did in his house when Jane, Candace and Sarah finished laying them out.

Even preparations for the school program were progressing. The *kinder* practiced their songs every morning until they knew them by heart. Amazingly, six-year-old Matthew Brenneman lost his shyness and showed a fine voice. To the child's delight, Danny gave him a solo.

The poetry recitations still needed more work, especially from Enoch and Ben, but Hope had finally memorized her lines for the play. She still relied heavily on Bridget for moral support. Bridget sat behind the quilt curtain, ready to supply her a line if needed. It amazed Danny that the five-year-old had learned them all by heart since she couldn't read. The walls of the school gained examples of the student winter artwork until they covered nearly every surface.

Having missed their lunch because of their last prank, the Yoder twins remained well-behaved, much to Danny's amazement. Clearly, they'd gained respect for Ben. While things were going well at school, it was when he returned home each night that he grappled with his growing longing for Jane.

Every time he stepped through the door and saw her bustling about the house like a *frau*, the sight reminded him painfully of what might have been. She wasn't a wife waiting to welcome him home, but a dear friend that he'd give anything to see happy even as it broke his heart.

How could he convince her to stay?

Please, Gott, show me what to do.

Chapter Fifteen

Jane took her creations to Meriwether's store in the afternoons while Bridget stayed with Danny at school or with Eva. Her purse grew fatter. With Christmas only a week away, she needed to earn as much as possible before the demand dried up. She stayed later each night at Danny's trying to finish as many as possible. He joined her, helping bundle together the sprigs that she then wired to the frames. The closeness of their time together gave her hope that their friendship remained strong, but it made it harder to keep her feelings hidden.

Late in the week she made another trip to the balsam fir grove to replenish her supply, alone this time. Everywhere she walked in the woods, she saw memories of her time there with Danny, the snowball fight, her ignoble falls, his laughter. Her biggest regret remained not letting him kiss her that day. She could have had that memory to keep her company during the long years ahead.

On Friday, Mr. Meriwether checked the price of a bus ticket to her former hometown in Upstate New York on his computer at the store. The biweekly local bus would be going south on Christmas Eve morning. A dozen more sales, and she'd have enough to leave plus extra to start a new life. Her plan was coming together.

Jane wanted to feel relief, but the only emotion in her heart was sadness. She dreaded leaving Danny. If she didn't go soon, she might not have the courage to leave at all.

Eva helped Jane sew dresses from the deep blue material she'd bought with her first money. The pedal-operated sewing machine Eva owned turned out to be exactly like the one Jane learned on as a child. She spent an enjoyable afternoon sitting in front of the living room window chatting happily with Eva as they stitched together the pieces that would become Jane's first visible step back into the Amish faith. Her baptism in her old community would complete her journey.

After finishing the dresses and *kapps*, Jane called Bridget in from playing outside. Danny, Willis and Harley had been supervising sled rides down the hillside behind the forge. They came in with the youngsters. Holly plopped down by the stove, panting hard.

Jane hid the prayer cap behind her back. "Bridget, I have a present for you."

Bridget's eyes lit up. "For me? It's not my birthday yet."

They would celebrate Bridget's sixth birthday on Christmas Day in a new community among strangers, but they would be Amish folks. Jane prayed they would be as welcoming as the people of New Covenant had been.

"It's not for your birthday, but it's something you've wanted." Jane whipped out the pleated white *kapp* with pristine ribbons.

"It's beautiful." Bridget took it reverently. "Does this mean I'm Amish like Maddie and Hope?"

"*Ja*, we are both going to be Amish now. Come into the bedroom and I'll show you how to bundle up your hair under the *kapp*. Only God and a husband should see a woman's crowning glory."

Jane caught Danny's eye as he stood beside the door. The look on his face said he remembered brushing her hair the night she arrived at his home. She smiled softly and nodded once, thankful that he had been the one to see it.

On Sunday afternoon, Jane waited anxiously in Eva's living room for Bishop Schultz to arrive as she reviewed the eighteen articles of the *Dordrecht Confession*, the basis for the foundation of the church. Learning them during her baptismal preparation classes years ago didn't mean she could recite them now. When she faced her former bishop and asked to be baptized into his church, she would need to prove her sincerity. She waited with mixed feelings for Bishop Schultz to arrive. If he felt she was ready, she could face her new congregation with confidence.

Closing her eyes, she mouthed the words until one section eluded her. "Oh, I know it. What comes next?"

"Do you need Bridget to feed you the line?"

Jane looked up to find Danny watching her. The soft light in his eyes threatened to melt her heart on the spot. She focused instead on the page in front of her. "I keep forgetting this part."

"That's because you're trying too hard."

"I need to know this before Bishop Schultz gets here. Any suggestions, Teacher?"

He took a seat across from her. "You can write the answers on your arm the way Felix Yoder did for his last test."

Shocked, Jane pressed a hand to her chest. "He cheated?"

"That may have been his intention, but he was so nervous about getting caught that he broke out in a sweat and the ink blurred. He confessed the whole thing before taking the test."

"What did you do?"

"Felix and I spoke to his father, then I gave him an oral test. Turned out that writing the answers down actually helped him learn them. He passed."

"Are you suggesting I cheat, or is this story meant to dissuade me from cheating?"

He winked at her. "Take it as a cautionary tale and use waterproof ink."

She chuckled and rolled her eyes. "You're not helping."

"I'm keeping your mind off your worst-case scenarios. You'll be fine."

"How can you be so sure?"

"Because I know how much you want this. For yourself and for Bridget."

"I do want it. I'm ready." Jane closed her eyes and took a deep breath, grateful for his support.

"*Goot*, because the bishop is outside."

Jane shot to her feet. Danny took the book from her trembling fingers. "I'll be right here when you're finished."

Those comforting words brought tears to her eyes. The thought of leaving Danny became harder to bear with each passing day. If only she could stay.

Nodding her thanks, she met the bishop in

the kitchen. His kind, reassuring demeanor dispelled the last of her concerns. After spending thirty minutes answering his questions and sharing her feelings about why she left and why she wished to return to the faith, she gained a deeper understanding of the commitment she was going to make.

"Thank you, Bishop." Jane knew in her heart that returning to her Amish faith was part of God's plan for her.

Danny peeked around the doorway from the living room. The bishop chuckled when he caught sight of him. "Come in, Danny."

"She'll make a fine Amish woman, won't she?" Danny's confident assertion made Jane smile.

The bishop nodded. "She will. I've had an answer to my letter from Bishop Barkman. Jane, you and Bridget are welcome to settle in his community."

Jane glanced at Danny to share her relief. Grief filled his eyes for an instant before he forced a smile. A stab of pain cut her heart at his sorrow.

"They will be blessed to have you both." He left the house and didn't return for supper that evening.

The following day, Jane carried the lunch she'd made for Bridget and Danny to the school.

She had to tell him she was leaving on Christmas Eve morning. It would be one of the hardest things she'd ever done, but she couldn't put it off any longer.

Inside, she saw Danny had implemented her suggestion for stage curtains. A rope stretched across one corner of the room. Two lovely quilts provided screens the actors could wait behind until their turn on stage. They could be drawn closed until the play was set to begin.

Maddie and Enoch kneeled beside a makeshift manger. As Jane watched, Hope walked from behind the curtain toward them. She stopped and looked back. "What's my line?"

"The baby looks cold," Bridget said in a loud whisper from her place at a desk in the audience.

Prompted by Bridget, Hope delivered her lines in a soft-spoken voice.

"Hope, honey, you're going to have to speak up," Sarah coached from her place behind the curtain.

Hope shouted her line at the top of her voice. Jane heard a smothered snicker behind her and turned to see Danny sitting at the back of the room. She walked over and settled in the seat beside him.

"It's going well, I see." She tried to keep a straight face but failed.

He wiped a hand across his mouth. "This may end up being the funniest program we've ever given if I'm not crying by the end."

She tried to be optimistic. "It's going to take a little more practice. There's still time."

Leaning forward, he propped his elbows on the desktop. "What brings you here?"

"I came to drop off your lunch. You forgot it this morning."

"Maybe I forgot it on purpose so that you would feel compelled to visit me."

"Did you?" She wished it were true and then chided herself for the foolish thought.

He sighed heavily and dropped his chin onto his crossed arms. "*Nee*, I've been worried and distracted about this rehearsal. I appreciate you bringing it. Are you taking Bridget back to the house with you?"

"I'll see if she wants to go."

He stood up. "Scholars, it's time for lunch."

The children left their places on stage and went to collect their lunch boxes. Then they gathered in groups in different parts of the school, boys on one side, and girls on the other, except for Otto and Candace, who sat together.

Jane tipped her head toward them. "Is there a schoolroom romance looming here?"

"I hope not. Otto is too young to have his heart broken."

"That sounds cynical."

"It's what usually happens to romances that start at school." Danny's gaze remained fixed on her face. She looked away.

Bridget came over to sit beside her. "What's for lunch?"

"Ham sandwich and a cup of tomato with rice soup."

"Yum, my favorite," Danny said.

"Mine, too." Bridget shouted.

Jane opened the lunch box. "Do you want to come back to the house with me?"

Bridget hesitated. "No, I'm going to stay here. Hope needs me to help her with her lines."

Jane avoided looking at Danny. She didn't want the memory of his pain. "I'm going to the bus station after I see Mr. Meriwether and get our tickets. I have enough money now. We'll be leaving Christmas Eve morning for our new life in New York."

She heard Danny's sharp intake of breath. Looking his way, she read the shock on his face.

Bridget glowered at her. "We can't leave before the Christmas program. Hope needs me to help her."

Jane took Bridget's hands in hers. "I'm sorry. You know why we must leave." Albert wasn't due back until after the first of the year, but Jane wanted to be long gone before that happened. Danny got to his feet and moved away. She wanted to comfort him but knew there was nothing she could say.

"Please don't make me leave my friends, Auntie Jane. I want to stay here. Can't we get a house in New Covenant?" Bridget's pleading eyes cut into Jane's heart.

"I wish we could." Thoughts of leaving Danny sat like a stone on her chest. "We must leave before Albert gets back."

"Maybe he doesn't want us to live with him anymore. Couldn't we ask him if it's okay to live in a different house?"

Jane pulled Bridget into a tight hug. If only it were that easy.

Bridget pushed away from Jane and ran to Danny. "Teacher, tell Auntie Jane you don't want us to leave. Make her to stay."

Anguish twisted Jane's heart at the pain in his eyes. He picked up Bridget. She wrapped her arms around his neck. "Okay. Jane, please stay."

"I can't. Please don't ask again." She couldn't bear the pleading in his eyes. Battling back tears, she ran out of the building. Danny called her name, but she didn't stop.

Reaching the house, she closed the door and leaned against it trying to shut out the disappointment in Danny's eyes. Danny and Bridget wanted her to stay in New Covenant. Bridget didn't realize how impossible that was, but Danny did.

Drying her tears on the corner of her apron, she walked to her craft table. She needed to finish another half dozen this afternoon. Dropping onto her chair, she stared at the vibrant green foliage wishing she could let Danny know she didn't want to go.

"Please, Lord, I know you are with me. Give me the strength to do what I must."

Sighing heavily, she picked up a bundle of holly and got to work.

A little before two o'clock someone knocked at Danny's front door. Surprised, Jane got up and pulled aside the curtain to peek out. An English fellow she didn't recognize waited with his shoulders hunched against the cold. Should she let him in? If he was a friend of Danny, it wasn't right to leave him standing outside.

She opened the door. "Is Danny about?" He had a friendly smile.

"He hasn't returned from school yet. I expect him any minute. Won't you come in?" She nervously stepped back from the door, wishing she hadn't answered his knock.

"Thank you." Moving into the living room, he stopped short at the sight of her wreaths. "I see why the house smells like Christmas. You must be the one making the greenery Meriwether has for sale at his store."

"I am."

"I've purchased a dozen already to decorate my church."

Holly dashed out of her box in the kitchen, barking happily. Bridget burst through the front door. "Auntie Jane. Guess what I drew in school?"

Three of her niece's artistic efforts already adorned the front of Danny's refrigerator. They were all the same subject. "A drawing of Holly?"

"Nope. It's a picture of Hope in her costume with a broken wing." Bridget held up her paper. Then she spied the man waiting to see Danny. She immediately hid behind Jane. "Who is that?" she whispered.

He smiled cheerfully. "I'm a friend of your teacher. My name is Frank Pearson, and who are you?"

Alarm bells went off in Jane's brain. Why did she know the name?

Bridget peeked around Jane. "I'm Bridget."

His smile faded. "Would you be Bridget Christner?"

"Yup."

Jane's heart dropped. He knew. She read it in his eyes.

"And this must be your aunt Jane. People looking for the two of you."

The outside door opened. Danny came in. He stopped short at the sight of his visitor. "Frank. What are you doing here?"

"I've been visiting a sick parishioner. Since I was passing by, I thought I'd give you an update on the missing Christner family. But I see you already know more than I do. How long have they been staying with you?"

Danny moved to Jane's side. The wild look in her eyes told him she was ready to take Bridget and run. "They've been staying with Eva. Jane works here during the day while I teach."

He indicated for Frank to take a seat on the sofa and sat beside him. Jane picked up Bridget and held her close.

Frank smiled at Jane. "I'm not an enforcement officer. I can't remove Bridget from your care. Please, sit down. Let's talk this over."

Jane crossed to stand with her back against the fireplace. "I won't let her go back to Albert. She isn't safe with him."

"Understood. Let's discuss what can be done."

Danny leaned forward and propped his elbows on his knees. "They have been living in an abusive situation. Jane is right, Bridget isn't safe with Albert. How do we get her away from him?"

"I have a way," Jane glared at Danny.

Frank leaned back and crossed his legs. "Custody cases are tricky and frequently messy. Because Danny asked me to get involved, and I'm a licensed social worker, I already know something about the situation. I need to hear your side of the story, Jane. Please have a seat. Bridget, is this your puppy?"

Holly came over to investigate the stranger. He ruffled her ears. She stood on her back legs and put her front paws on his knee.

"That's Holly," Bridget said. "We gave her to Danny."

"Jane wants to become Bridget's guardian. How can she do that?" Danny asked.

Frank latched his fingers around his knee. "A change of custody is possible, but it isn't something that happens quickly. There's an open case on Bridget so that will speed things up, but guardianship is decided by a court of law. Albert's refusal to meet with the child welfare people is a strike against him."

Danny glanced at Jane and then back to Frank. "Bishop Scholz suggested we get an attorney."

Frank nodded. "That is exactly what you should do."

"I don't have a home. I don't have a job. Will they give me custody of Bridget?" Some of the panic had left her eyes.

"That is not an ideal situation, but you are a relative—that's in your favor. Child services will want to do a home inspection before placing a child anywhere. The accusation of neglect will have to be investigated."

"My uncle is working in Bangor until after the first of the year. If they prove he neglected her, she stays with me, right?"

"Yes, but it's likely that she will be placed in social service custody until the issue can be resolved. It shouldn't be more than a few days before you are granted temporary custody. A few weeks at most."

"No. She's not going into foster care. Not for a few weeks, not even for a few days. She stays with me."

Frank held up both hands. "I understand your feelings, but the wheels of justice can move slowly."

Danny leaned back in his chair. "If Jane and Bridget have a home and means of support, will that speed up the process?"

"Certainly."

Danny got up and took Bridget from Jane's hold. He kneeled to speak to her. "I want you to go over and play with Maddie for a while."

She smiled happily. "Okay. Can Holly come with me?"

"Sure."

Bridget went out the door with the puppy. Danny rose to face Jane. "May I speak to you privately for a moment? Excuse us, Frank."

In the kitchen, Danny sat down across from Jane at the table and took a deep breath. "Hear me out before you answer."

"All right."

"There's a way I can help you to keep Bridget."

"I'm listening."

"Marry me."

Danny cringed as Jane jerked back. He shouldn't have sprung it on her so suddenly.

He rushed on. "Think about the advantages. I have a home for you and Bridget. I have a job that will support both of you. Bishop Schultz said you are ready to join the church—join it here. He'll agree to marry us once you do."

She stared at him without blinking.

This wasn't going well. "I don't need an answer straightaway. Think about it. You and I get along, Jane. We're friends. My family loves you. Bridget likes me. Even Holly likes me." He tried to lighten the moment. When she didn't smile, his hopes sank.

He reached across and took her hand. "I'm willing to listen to your feelings on the subject."

Chapter Sixteen

What were her feelings? Other than shock, Jane couldn't find a reaction to share with him. "Are you serious?"

"Marriages have started off with less in common. We both love Bridget and want her to be safe and happy."

He offered her marriage not because he loved her, but because he loved Bridget. What a brave and utterly selfless act. It solved everything. Bridget would have a home. Danny would care for her and love her; Jane knew it without a doubt. Could she face a lifetime of marriage to a man who didn't love her, but would sacrifice everything for her little girl?

Jane pulled her hand away from Danny and laced her fingers together. Why was she hesitating? What option did she have except to leave and hope they wouldn't be found in New York?

"Bridget is happy here," he said softly.

She glanced out the window where Bridget, Hope and Maddie, along with Holly, were frolicking on the playground equipment. Was she wrong to tear Bridget away from the first genuine happiness she'd known? "Every day, the horrors of the last few years are falling away from her."

"What about you? Are you letting go of the past?"

"I don't have that luxury."

"Then let me give it to you. Let me give you safety, security, a home of your own."

But not love.

Danny cared about her. That was clear. He was her friend, but was that enough to sustain them through fifty or sixty years of marriage? Bridget would grow up, perhaps marry, even move away to start her own family, and leave Jane with what, exactly? The Amish faith she was ready to embrace didn't allow divorce. If she agreed to Danny's proposal, it would be forever. To a man who didn't love her.

She couldn't let him to do it.

He deserved to marry a woman he loved with his whole generous heart and who loved him unconditionally. The way she loved him. And that was why she couldn't accept his offer.

Gathering her courage, she shook her head. "Danny, I can't marry you."

Disappointment flashed across his face as the hope in his eyes faded. He stared at the tabletop then nodded slowly. "I understand."

He drew a shaky breath and stood. "I'll have Frank find an attorney for you. I'll pay for it. It's the least I can do for Bridget."

He walked out of the kitchen with slumped shoulders. Jane laid her head on her arms at the table and wept silent tears.

Later that afternoon, Jane walked the short mile to Mr. Meriwether's store, needing time to clear her head. She'd made the right choice, so why did it feel as if she'd lost her chance at happiness? If only Danny loved her as she loved him, she would have said yes in a heartbeat.

Lilly Arnett stood at the counter speaking to Mr. Meriwether. Jane waited patiently until she finished. The woman walked toward Jane, tucking her wallet into her purse.

"Merry Christmas, Lilly." Jane tried for a friendly smile despite the ache in her heart.

Lilly stopped. "I was telling Lou that your uncle is not a nice man. I'm sorry—I know he's your relation, but he had the gall to show up at my place and demand more money for his cow because I didn't pay him what she was worth.

Can you believe that? He set the price. The man's a liar and a cheat."

Jane tried to concentrate on Lilly's face as darkness narrowed her vision. A buzzing filled her ears. "You spoke to Albert?"

"This morning."

"He isn't supposed to return for two more weeks." Why had he come back now? In two days she and Bridget would be on a bus bound for Upstate New York and safe from him.

Mr. Meriwether came over. "Albert was in here not thirty minutes ago and in a foul mood. He asked if I'd seen you. I told him you were staying with the Amish."

The wreaths fell out of Jane's arms. "Bridget!"

Lilly reached for Jane. "You're pale as a sheet. What's wrong?"

"He'll take my baby." She stumbled toward the door desperate to reach Bridget.

"Don't you want to be paid for these?" Mr. Meriwether called out.

Running for what seemed like forever, Jane finally reached the bend in the road near the school and saw Bridget playing with Holly, Maddie and Hope. They were building a snowman while Danny watched. Her baby was safe.

Jane pressed her hand against the painful stitch in her side and staggered forward. Danny caught sight of her and rushed toward her. He must've seen the panic in her eyes because he broke into a run.

"What is it? What's wrong?"

Gripping his arms, she tried to catch her breath. "Albert's back."

"It's okay. Calm down." Danny pulled her against him. "He doesn't know you're here."

"He does. Mr. Meriwether told him."

A brown car careened past them and skidded to a stop on the roadway near where the girls were playing with the puppy. Albert got out and charged toward them. Holly barked furiously. Albert grabbed Hope and pulled back her bonnet. Maddie and Bridget tugged on his arm, screaming at him. Danny ran toward the girls. Jane staggered after him.

Albert released Hope and grabbed Bridget. Holly nipped at his heels. He kicked at the pup, but she dodged his blow. Bridget screamed. Alfred reached his car and shoved her in before Danny could stop him.

He sped away, weaving wildly down the highway.

Danny bent over with his hands on his knees. "I'm sorry, Jane, I couldn't stop him."

Jane collapsed in the snow. *Dear God, this can't be happening.*

Otto came running from the smithy. "I saw him take her. What do we do?"

Danny stood upright. "Run to the phone shack and call 9-1-1. Tell them a child has been abducted from the school. Call Bishop Schultz's business. Tell him Albert has taken Bridget and what kind of car Albert is driving. The bishop's business is on the highway toward Fort Craig. Ask him to keep a lookout for it." The boy took off.

Danny helped Jane to her feet. "I need you to stay here and talk to the police when they arrive."

"Where are you going?"

"To the cabin. Where else would he go?"

She clutched his arm, drawing strength from him. "I'm coming with you."

Maddie had run in to get Willis and Eva. They gathered close. "What can we do?" Willis asked.

Jane pressed a hand to her forehead. It was hard to think. "Tell the police what happened, but don't mention that Albert is her guardian. They may not look for her if they know."

Danny drew her into an embrace. Jane pressed her face against his neck. "We have to find her."

He held her tight. "We will. *Gott* is with her. He is our strength."

A pickup pulled to a stop on the road. Lilly

got out with Mr. Meriwether. "You frightened us, Jane. What's going on?"

Maddie kicked a lump of snow. "That mean man took Bridget."

Lilly's eyebrows shot up. "She's been abducted? Have you called the police?"

Jane forced herself to move away from the safety of Danny's arms. "Otto ran to the phone. They should be here soon. Lilly, can you drive us to the cabin?"

"Sure. Get in." She ran around to the driver's side.

Mr. Meriwether opened the door for Jane and Danny. "I'll wait here. I have some information the police may want. Albert had been drinking heavily."

"Call me on my cell phone if you hear anything, Lou." Lilly started the engine.

"I will." He shut the door.

She sped to the edge of town and turned off into the forest on the snow-packed track. Jane held on to Danny and prayed. It took forever to reach the farm. Jane imagined every moment how scared Bridget must be.

"His car isn't here." Lilly stopped in front of the cabin.

Jane jumped out to search the house while Danny went to the barn. She called for Bridget as she went through the house but met only silence. She saw at once that Albert had taken everything of value from the place. He wasn't coming back.

Outside, she saw Danny shake his head as he came out of the barn. Jane bit down on her knuckle. Where was Albert? "Where has he taken my baby?"

Danny wrapped his arms around her. They clung to each other without speaking.

Lilly touched Jane's arm. "Let me take you home."

Jane looked into Danny's eyes. "I can't go home without her. She's scared, Danny. I want her in my arms. Why is this happening?"

"We can't know why, but *Gott* is with her, and He is with us. We must accept His will. Let's go back. The police may know something by now."

Jane allowed him to help her into the truck. She leaned against him drawing comfort from his arm curved protectively over her shoulders and she prayed.

Lilly dropped them at Eva's house as the evening shadows blurred day into dusk. Lights shone from every window. Danny saw a dozen buggies in the schoolyard. Lights shone from those windows, too. Word had gotten around.

The front door opened. Eva came running out. "Anything?"

Danny shook his head. "We were hoping you had heard something."

"Nothing." Eva embraced Jane and led her to the house. A handful of women waited for them on the porch. They surrounded Jane and bundled her inside.

Danny wanted her back in his arms, but he knew she needed the comfort of the community. His abject failure to protect Bridget pulled him down. Jane might forgive him, but how could he forgive himself?

Please, merciful Father, bring our child home safe.

Bridget was the child of his heart. He loved her more than words could express. He and Jane would forever share that bond no matter what happened, or how far away she moved. They were the people he loved most in the world. Why hadn't he told them that?

Sighing heavily, he shoved his hands in his coat pockets. It wouldn't have made a difference. Jane didn't love him. Some flaw in his character made him unlovable.

He turned to walk to his empty house but heard Willis calling him and changed direction. Willis stood at the door to the forge. Danny stepped inside. The glowing coals had the building toasty warm.

"The police asked me to stay here and coordinate things on our end. Harley and some of the men are out looking for Albert's car on the backroads. A few of the teenage boys have cell phones. Harley left me his so I can notify them if the police find anything."

Danny pulled off his hat and raked his hand through his hair. "Albert could be miles away by now."

"Or he could be hiding in someone's barn or hunting cabin waiting until dark. No one knows these woods better than our men. We'll find him."

"I pray you're right." As much as Danny's heart ached for Bridget, it ached more for the pain Jane endured each minute Albert had Bridget. "I need to do something. I should be out searching. It's my fault he got away." He started for the door.

Willis caught his arm. "You can't think like that."

Eva came in to join them. Danny took a step toward her. "How's Jane?"

"Holding up. Barely. Everyone is praying with her." Eva drew a deep breath. "Once she has Bridget back, we all want her to settle here. Bethany and Michael intend to let her have their cottage rent-free for a year. The bishop's wife says he will hire her as a secretary at his business. Do you think we can change her mind about going to New York?"

Danny settled his hat on his head. "I don't know."

Eva looked surprised. "That sounds glum. I thought you'd be at the front of the line asking her to stay. It's obvious how you feel about her."

"I did ask. She turned me down."

Willis crossed his arms and frowned. "What are you saying?"

Danny braced himself to reveal the humiliating truth. "I asked Jane to marry me. I offered her a home and security so she could apply to become Bridget's guardian. She turned me down."

Willis's eyes filled with sympathy. "Oh, Danny. I'm so sorry. I don't understand why. The woman can't keep her eyes off you."

"She doesn't love me." It hurt to admit the truth out loud.

Eva shook her head. "I can't believe she said that."

"She didn't have to say it. I thought keeping her and Bridget together would be enough for her, but it wasn't."

Eva narrowed her gaze. "You offered to marry her so she could keep Bridget?"

"*Ja*, Frank Pearson said it would make it easier for her to get custody."

Taking a step back, Eva tipped her head to the side. "You mentioned how much you love her, right?"

"She knows I love Bridget."

"But did you tell Jane that you love Jane, too?" Eva bit out each word.

Danny flinched. "You said it's obvious. Why else would I ask her to marry me?"

Willis smacked a hand to his forehead. "You have a lot to learn about women. No wonder she refused you."

Eva cupped Danny's cheeks between her hands. "What do you want, little *brudder*?"

What he couldn't have. "I want Jane for my wife and Bridget for my daughter. Nothing would make me happier. I love them with my whole heart, but more than that I want Bridget back safely in Jane's arms."

"Does Jane love you?" Eva asked gently.

"I don't know." Was it possible he had misunderstood her reason for refusing him?

Willis gripped his shoulder. "Don't you think you should find out?"

Danny's biggest fear loomed before him. "What if she doesn't?"

Eva poked a finger in Danny's chest. "When this is over, ask her. After you tell her you love her and can't imagine life without her." She spun around in frustration. "Why don't we hear something?"

The door opened. Lilly poked her head in. "The police have found her. Come on. Jane's already in my truck."

By the dome light of Lilly's pickup, Jane saw the relief in her heart reflected in Danny's eyes as he joined her. He grasped her hand in a reassuring grip. "I knew *Gott* would not let us down."

"Everyone was praying with me. It was wonderfully comforting. *Gott* is great." She smiled at his beloved face and saw something else in his eyes. A tenderness she had longed for.

Danny squeezed her fingers. "I need to talk to you later. After we have our little girl safe."

He didn't release her hand as Lilly drove them to the outskirts of Fort Craig where three police cruisers with red lights flashing in the darkness sat along the road. Albert's car was down in the ditch. As soon as Lilly stopped, Danny jumped out of the vehicle. Jane followed and ran toward the officers. "Where's Bridget? Where is she?"

One man stepped away from the other. He touched the brim of his hat. "Evening, ma'am. I'm Officer Melvin Peaks of the Maine State Police."

"I'm Jane Christner. Where is my niece, Bridget?"

"Over here." He led her to the first cruiser. He opened the rear door.

Bridget, seated beside a young female officer, caught sight of Jane and squealed as she launched herself into Jane's arms. Jane held her small warm body close and gave thanks to God that she was safe. Danny encircled them both in hug Jane never wanted to end.

The young woman got out of the car. "I'm sorry this happened, but she seems fine."

Officer Peaks stepped away to answer the radio.

The woman stroked Bridget's hair. "He keeps claiming he's her legal guardian, but he doesn't know her birthday or even her age."

Jane's chin quivered. Danny kissed her temple. "It's all right. We must tell them," he whispered. "No more hiding. No more deceptions."

He was right. She had put her trust in God's mercy, and He brought Bridget back to her. Jane looked at the woman. "Albert is her guardian, but he's an abusive man. I took Bridget and ran away to protect her."

Officer Peaks came back and nodded toward Albert in the backseat of the nearby police cruiser. "He has two outstanding warrants in Bangor. We're taking him in. He'll be charged with DWI and criminal endangerment of a child. The breathalyzer shows he's legally intoxicated. He was speeding, and she wasn't in a child car seat."

"Can I go home now, Auntie Jane?" Bridget asked.

Jane looked at the officer. "May we take her home?"

"Of course." He nodded toward Albert. "He's going to be in jail for a while."

A white sedan pulled up behind them. A middle-aged woman got out. She held out a name badge. "Officer Peaks, I'm Melissa Fredericks with the offices of Child and Family Services. I was told you have a child in need of care?"

"We did but her family arrived."

Melissa smiled and held out her hand. "You must be Jane. I'm very glad to meet you. I've had a long conversation with Pastor Pearson. You don't have anything to worry about. Bridget may stay with you until the court appoints you as her new guardian. We're just happy she's safe."

Jane's knees threatened to buckle. Danny held her up. She tried to thank Melissa, but she broke down in tears instead.

Chapter Seventeen

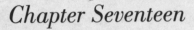

Danny popped into Eva's kitchen the next morning. Jane smiled at him, the light in her eyes giving him hope. Was it only happiness at having Bridget safe or was there something else? What if she didn't love him? What if she still wanted to move away? There were so many questions that needed answering.

What if she did love him?

"Have a seat." Eva dished up scrambled eggs.

"I can't stay. I have too much to do at the school before the program tomorrow. I wanted to see that everyone is okay. Bridget, how are you?"

"I'm fine, but Jane says I can't go to school today."

Jane straightened Bridget's *kapp* and tugged the ribbons. "I need you close."

"How are you, Jane?" The urge to take her in

his arms was overpowering. How was it possible to love someone so much?

A wry smile curved her pretty mouth. "Recovering."

"*Goot.* I should go." Before he blurted out how much he loved her in front of everyone.

"Last night you said you needed to speak to me." She waited for his reply.

Danny glanced around the room full of people. "Later."

"Oh." She sounded disappointed. "Okay."

He escaped the disapproving looks of Eva and Willis and headed to school. There was a lot to do, but he had a hard time concentrating. All he could think about was telling Jane he loved her and asking if she loved him, too.

If the children sensed his inattention, they didn't mention it. The final rehearsal for the program went well, but Hope complained of feeling sick. Sarah assured her it was only nerves and she'd feel fine once the play started.

When he finally dismissed the students for the day, he stepped outside and caught sight of a splotch of red and white on his porch. When he got closer, he realized Jane was sitting on his steps wrapped in the star quilt his sister had made for him. The one he'd wrapped her in the first night she came to his home.

His heart turned over. The one thing he wanted

for Christmas sat on his doorstep. If Jane didn't return his feelings, he had no idea how he could go on. It required more courage than he knew he possessed to walk up and sit down beside her.

Steam rose from the mug she had clasped between her hands, filling the cold air with the enticing aroma of freshly brewed coffee.

"What are you doing out here?"

She didn't meet his gaze. "Waiting for you."

His hopes rose. "You could wait in the warm house."

"You said you had needed to talk to me. I thought maybe Bridget shouldn't overhear. We don't have to sit out here. Come in. I'll get you a cup of coffee."

"*Nee*, I'm comfortable." He wasn't. He'd never been more anxious in his life. "The coffee smells *goot*."

"I'll get you a mug."

She started to rise, but he stopped her. "There's no need. A sip of yours will be enough. If you don't mind?"

She blushed a pretty shade of pink. "Of course not. It's your mug and your coffee."

"But your hands are holding it. Your lips have touched the brim. Fortunate coffee cup." He had no idea where those words came from.

She turned her face away and his heart sank. "I'm sorry. That was too bold of me. It's just that you mean so much to me, Jane. I've fallen in love with you."

She looked at him then. "You love me?"

"More than I can ever express."

"When you proposed, you didn't say anything about love."

He stared at his feet. "I should have. The truth is, I couldn't bear to hear that you didn't love me. Bridget has been the most important thing in the world to you since she was born. I desperately wanted the two of you to be safe and happy together. I didn't tell you how much I love you then, but I'm telling you now."

Danny fell silent, his heart pounding so hard he was sure she could hear it.

When she didn't say anything, he looked up. "Even if you don't feel the same, I needed to tell you that I love you and Bridget."

She held the cup toward him. "Danny Coblentz, I love you with my whole heart. I can't believe you love me, too. Do you really?"

He took the cup from her and set it on the porch step, pulled off his mittens and took her hands in his. "May I kiss you, Jane?"

Her eyes filled with relief, then her lips curved in a sweet smile. "*Ja*, you may."

Indescribable joy filled his being. Leaning toward her, he cupped her face with his hands and gently kissed her soft lips.

* * *

The warmth of Danny's lips pressed to hers sent a thrill to the center of Jane's heart where it exploded into overwhelming love. All she wanted was to be closer, to be held by him and cherished for a lifetime.

He broke the kiss, resting his forehead against hers. "I have wanted to do that for so long. Do you know how amazing you are?"

"I know that you make me feel incredible."

He pulled back to gaze into her eyes, his expression serious, worried even. "You don't have to be afraid anymore. You can go anywhere now."

"Or I can stay in New Covenant." She hoped he understood what she wanted to say. That she never wanted to leave him.

His expression softened. "I had no idea how incomplete I was until I met you and Bridget. I love you, Jane, with all my heart and soul."

She squeezed his hands. "I've been in love with you since the moment I saw you playing on the school grounds with Sadie Sue. I heard you laugh and something inside me burst into life. I didn't know it was love then, but I know it now. The Lord fashioned you to complete me."

The joy in his eyes sent her heart soaring. "Jane, will you marry me?"

She gazed at him intently. "To give Bridget a home?"

"*Nee*, to give my heart a home." He pulled her into his arms and pressed his cheek against hers. "I love you. I'll always love you and I'll never tire of telling you how much you mean to me."

"You rescued me. Not just from my cruel uncle, but from a life of despair and doubting the goodness of *Gott*."

He kissed her temple and drew back to gaze into her eyes. "You haven't answered my question. Will you marry me?"

"With a glad heart. When?"

A frown furrowed his brow. "I know these things take time. I remember Eva's wedding preparations. I can wait a few months."

"I don't need a big affair. I don't have family to invite. Once I'm baptized and the bishop reads our banns, I don't want to wait another day."

Danny stood up and pulled her to her feet. "I think you're the most wonderful woman in the world." He kissed her, sending her heart into fireworks once more. She had a second to wonder if it would always be like this before she heard a sharp intake of breath.

"Auntie Jane! Are you kissing the teacher?" Bridget's shocked expression brought Jane rashing back to reality. She hadn't considered how Bridget would react to this.

Danny slipped his arm around Jane's shoulder. "She is kissing the teacher and the teacher is kissing her back because we are in love. With each other, with you, with Holly and with our great and wonderful Lord who brought us all together. Is there any chance you would like to become my daughter?"

She considered his question longer than Jane liked. "Can I still go to school if you are my papa?"

He held out his arms. "Absolutely."

Bridget squealed and threw herself into his embrace. He held her and wrapped his other arm around Jane. "Little did I know that a stray puppy would bring the most amazing Christmas to my doorstep."

Jane pressed her face against his chest. "It's cold out here. Let's go in."

They walked up the steps together, and Danny knew he had found the family he longed for in the arms of a woman who loved him. *Gott* was indeed *goot*.

Epilogue

Danny paced in front of the school doors on Christmas Eve. The last of the crowd had arrived. The school was full. The children gathered behind the quilts that had been hung to screen off the stage. Everyone was there except Hope.

Jane came outside. "It's time to start."

His heart jumped in his chest at her nearness. He loved her so much. And wonder of wonders, she loved him, too. Her knowing smile proved she knew what he was thinking. He winked at her. "May I kiss you?"

She primly shook her head. "Like our announcement, that must wait until after the program."

They had agreed to delay telling everyone until the banns were read in church as was the Amish custom. This was the children's big night. They didn't want to take anything away from them. Bridget knew, of course, but had promised to keep their secret. Danny knew she was dying to tell Maddie and Hope.

A horse and buggy came trotting round the bend from the direction of the Crump farm. Danny pressed a hand to his chest. "Panic over. Here they come."

Jane laughed. The light in her eyes sparked a desire to sweep her into his arms. He pushed his hands down in his coat pockets.

She stepped back. "I'll have the children get ready."

He wanted to kiss her smiling lips, tell her again how much he loved her, but the Crumps' buggy turned into the parking lot. He went down the steps to greet them. "I was starting to worry."

Jesse got out of the buggy alone. Danny frowned. "Where's Hope?"

"She's running a fever. I'm sorry. Gemma sent her wings and gown for one of the other children to use when they take her place."

Danny managed a smile. *"Danki."*

Every child in school had a speaking part. There was no one left.

He carried the box into the school past the families and friends waiting eagerly for the performance. Stepping behind the curtain, he found all eyes on him.

"Hope is sick and won't be with us tonight. This is your play. I know how much work you've put into it, but I think we should cancel the performance."

Jane moved to his side. "Can't someone take her part? What about Maddie? She knows all the lines. She and Bridget have been practicing every night."

He turned to Maddie. "Could you do it?"

Maddie frowned. "Who will play Mary?"

He looked at Candace and Sarah. "What about one of you?"

Bridget tugged on his coat. "I can be Newest Angel."

"I'm sure you could, sweetheart, but you aren't one of our students."

Sarah looked around the group. "I think she should do it." The others nodded.

Danny handed Jane the box. "Why not? Everyone take your places."

He walked out to face the audience. "*Frehlicher Grischtdaag*, a merry Christmas to everyone and welcome. Hope Crump is ill and can't be with us tonight. The part of Newest Angel will be performed by Bridget Christner."

A smattering of applause broke out. Everyone had heard about Bridget's abduction and rescue.

Danny took a deep breath. "Let's start our program."

Jane pulled the quilt aside. The children lined up with Bridget standing in the first row wearing Hope's angel costume and a bright smile.

A round of applause followed each song. Annabeth recited her poem flawlessly. The two boys stumbled a little, but that didn't diminish the audience's appreciation for their efforts. Finally, it was time for the play. Danny looked at Jane. She smiled, gave a brief nod and pulled the quilts aside.

Sarah, Candace and Otto stood at center stage. Candace put her hands on her hips and began to list the problems they were having with Newest Angel. She was always late to meetings. She couldn't keep her gown clean, and she had broken her new wings.

Jane kneeled by Bridget. "Are you ready?"

Danny dropped to one knee beside them. "We have great faith in you, Bridget."

"We do," Jane added, smiling tenderly at him.

Bridget raised her chin. "I'm ready."

Turning around, she walked boldly out to stand in front of Otto. A twitter of laughter swept through the audience at the sight of her heavily smudged gown and crooked wing.

Danny laced his fingers through Jane's as they stood side by side behind the quilt. She smiled at him as her heart filled with happiness at the wonders God had wrought in her life. Chief among them was this kind, caring man who made her heart sing.

On stage, Otto grasped his hands behind his back and asked Newest Angel why she wasn't happy in heaven.

"I don't like it here. I want my blankie. Mamma made it for me. I've always had it. I can't go to sleep without it." She popped her thumb in her mouth.

Head Angel told her God had chosen a special assignment just for her hoping that would make her happy.

Bridget finished her lines and came behind the quilt. "Did I do okay?"

Danny gave her a quick hug. "You're doing great."

"That's because I know what it's like to sad and miss something special. Jane got my momma's picture book for me, and I was happy again."

Danny tilted his head to look at Jane. "She's an amazing woman."

"Yup. Can I tell Maddie our secret?" she whispered.

Jane shook her head. "Not yet."

Maddie carried a small stool out onto the stage and sat down. Bridget went out to join her dragging a chair. Laughter rippled through the audience.

She placed the chair beside Maddie, climbed on it and held her arms wide. "Hey, Mary. God thinks you're special. You're gonna have a baby."

When they finished the scene and came off stage, Maddie hugged Bridget. "You did great."

Danny held his finger to his lips. "Shush, we have more play."

As Candace, Sarah and Otto conferred on-stage about the trouble with Newest Angel and God's plan for her, Jane felt Danny slip his hand in hers. Was he thinking about God's plan for them? For their future? She gave his fingers a squeeze. They grinned at each other like guilty children. She couldn't wait to start their life together.

Newest Angel was given her blankie. Happy at last, she joined the other angels gathered around the newborn baby in the stable with the shepherds and kings. Newest Angel told Head Angel the baby in the manger looked cold. She gave Mary her blankie to swaddle the infant telling her the blanket was filled with love.

Touched by her unselfish gift, Head Angel picked up Newest Angel and announced that God had a brand-new set of wings waiting for her.

As the play concluded, the audience gave the players a lively round of applause. Danny walked out to face the audience. "Thank you for coming. We hope you enjoyed our program. There are refreshments at the back of the room."

The children dispersed to their families and to grab cookies and lemonade.

Alone behind the curtain, Jane smiled at Danny's look of relief. "You made it."

"But I'll have to do it again next year."

"We'll manage together."

He gave her a quick kiss. "With you at my side I can do anything."

Bridget hopped up and down. "Can I please tell Maddie now?"

Jane looked at Danny. He nodded. She removed Bridget's broken wing. "Okay."

"Yea."

Danny chuckled. "Maddie will tell her whole family. I say we have until Sunday before the entire community knows."

"Knowing Eva, we have until the day after tomorrow." Jane didn't mind. She wanted everyone to know about the love they shared.

Bridget ran to the front of the stage. Maddie stood at the back of the room with Eva and Willis. The room reverberated with chatter. Bridget cupped her hands around her mouth. "Maddie, I have a secret to tell you."

"What is it?" Maddie called out.

Jane looked at Danny. "Oh, no."

"Teacher is going to marry Auntie Jane," Bridget yelled.

The whole room fell silent. Jane clapped her hands over her mouth. Danny cringed. They looked at each other, started laughing and fell into each other's arms as their smiling friends surged toward them.

* * * * *

Dear Reader,

I hope you've enjoyed this trip back to New Covenant, Maine. So many of my old characters popped in to say hello, I almost lost count of them.

It has been a trying year for me. I lost my father. Due to COVID restrictions I couldn't be with him when he passed. It broke my heart and bruised my spirit. I tested positive for COVID, too. While I wasn't very ill, the combination of all that happened left me struggling in my daily life. My writing suffered. I almost gave it up.

I want to thank my wonderful publisher, Harlequin, and my editor at Love Inspired, Emily Rodmell, for their compassion and understanding. It meant more than I can say that they adjusted my deadlines and allowed me the breathing room I needed. I have been blessed to write for such wonderful people.

I'm also blessed to have great readers. You have been my biggest inspiration. May the Lord bless you and keep you, this year and always. Merry Christmas.

Blessing,
Patricia Davids

Get 4 FREE REWARDS!

We'll send you 2 FREE Books plus 2 FREE Mystery Gifts.

FREE
Value Over
$20

Both the **Love Inspired**® and **Love Inspired**® **Suspense** series feature compelling novels filled with inspirational romance, faith, forgiveness, and hope.

YES! Please send me 2 FREE novels from the Love Inspired or Love Inspired Suspense series and my 2 FREE gifts (gifts are worth about $10 retail). After receiving them, if I don't wish to receive any more books, I can return the shipping statement marked "cancel." If I don't cancel, I will receive 6 brand-new Love Inspired Larger-Print books or Love Inspired Suspense Larger-Print books every month and be billed just $6.24 each in the U.S. or $6.49 each in Canada. That is a savings of at least 17% off the cover price. It's quite a bargain! Shipping and handling is just 50¢ per book in the U.S. and $1.25 per book in Canada.* I understand that accepting the 2 free books and gifts places me under no obligation to buy anything. I can always return a shipment and cancel at any time by calling the number below. The free books and gifts are mine to keep no matter what I decide.

Choose one: ☐ **Love Inspired**
Larger-Print
(122/322 IDN GRDF)

☐ **Love Inspired Suspense**
Larger-Print
(107/307 IDN GRDF)

Name (please print)

Address   Apt. #

City   State/Province   Zip/Postal Code

Email: Please check this box ☐ if you would like to receive newsletters and promotional emails from Harlequin Enterprises ULC and its affiliates. You can unsubscribe anytime.

Mail to the Harlequin Reader Service:
IN U.S.A.: P.O. Box 1341, Buffalo, NY 14240-8531
IN CANADA: P.O. Box 603, Fort Erie, Ontario L2A 5X3

Want to try 2 free books from another series? Call 1-800-873-8635 or visit www.ReaderService.com.

*Terms and prices subject to change without notice. Prices do not include sales taxes, which will be charged (if applicable) based on your state or country of residence. Canadian residents will be charged applicable taxes. Offer not valid in Quebec. This offer is limited to one order per household. Books received may not be as shown. Not valid for current subscribers to the Love Inspired or Love Inspired Suspense series. All orders subject to approval. Credit or debit balances in a customer's account(s) may be offset by any other outstanding balance owed by or to the customer. Please allow 4 to 6 weeks for delivery. Offer available while quantities last.

Your Privacy—Your information is being collected by Harlequin Enterprises ULC, operating as Harlequin Reader Service. For a complete summary of the information we collect, how we use this information and to whom it is disclosed, please visit our privacy notice located at corporate.harlequin.com/privacy-notice. From time to time we may also exchange your personal information with reputable third parties. If you wish to opt out of this sharing of your personal information, please visit readerservice.com/consumerschoice or call 1-800-873-8635. **Notice to California Residents**—Under California law, you have specific rights to control and access your data. For more information on these rights and how to exercise them, visit corporate.harlequin.com/california-privacy.

LIRLIS22R2

Get 4 FREE REWARDS!

We'll send you 2 FREE Books plus 2 FREE Mystery Gifts.

FREE
Value Over
$20

Both the **Harlequin® Special Edition** and **Harlequin® Heartwarming™** series feature compelling novels filled with stories of love and strength where the bonds of friendship, family and community unite.

YES! Please send me 2 FREE novels from the Harlequin Special Edition or Harlequin Heartwarming series and my 2 FREE gifts (gifts are worth about $10 retail). After receiving them, if I don't wish to receive any more books, I can return the shipping statement marked "cancel." If I don't cancel, I will receive 6 brand-new Harlequin Special Edition books every month and be billed just $5.24 each in the U.S. or $5.99 each in Canada, a savings of at least 13% off the cover price or 4 brand-new Harlequin Heartwarming Larger-Print books every month and be billed just $5.99 each in the U.S. or $6.49 each in Canada, a savings of at least 20% off the cover price. It's quite a bargain! Shipping and handling is just 50¢ per book in the U.S. and $1.25 per book in Canada.* I understand that accepting the 2 free books and gifts places me under no obligation to buy anything. I can always return a shipment and cancel at any time by calling the number below. The free books and gifts are mine to keep no matter what I decide.

Choose one: ☐ **Harlequin Special Edition**
(235/335 HDN GRCQ)

☐ **Harlequin Heartwarming Larger-Print**
(161/361 HDN GRC3)

Name (please print)

Address   Apt. #

City   State/Province   Zip/Postal Code

Email: Please check this box ☐ if you would like to receive newsletters and promotional emails from Harlequin Enterprises ULC and its affiliates. You can unsubscribe anytime.

Mail to the **Harlequin Reader Service:**
IN U.S.A.: P.O. Box 1341, Buffalo, NY 14240-8531
IN CANADA: P.O. Box 603, Fort Erie, Ontario L2A 5X3

Want to try 2 free books from another series! Call 1-800-873-8635 or visit www.ReaderService.com.

*Terms and prices subject to change without notice. Prices do not include sales taxes, which will be charged (if applicable) based on your state or country of residence. Canadian residents will be charged applicable taxes. Offer not valid in Quebec. This offer is limited to one order per household. Books received may not be as shown. Not valid for current subscribers to the Harlequin Special Edition or Harlequin Heartwarming series. All orders subject to approval. Credit or debit balances in a customer's account(s) may be offset by any other outstanding balance owed by or to the customer. Please allow 4 to 6 weeks for delivery. Offer available while quantities last.

Your Privacy—Your information is being collected by Harlequin Enterprises ULC, operating as Harlequin Reader Service. For a complete summary of the information we collect, how we use this information and to whom it is disclosed, please visit our privacy notice located at corporate.harlequin.com/privacy-notice. From time to time we may also exchange your personal information with reputable third parties. If you wish to opt out of this sharing of your personal information, please visit readerservice.com/consumerschoice or call 1-800-873-8635. **Notice to California Residents**—Under California law, you have specific rights to control and access your data. For more information on these rights and how to exercise them, visit corporate.harlequin.com/california-privacy.

HSEHW22R2

THE 2022 LOVE INSPIRED CHRISTMAS COLLECTION

Buy 3 and get 1 FREE!

May all that is beautiful, meaningful and brings you joy be yours this holiday season...including this fun-filled collection featuring 24 Christmas stories. From tender holiday romances to Christmas Eve suspense, this collection has it all.

COMING NEXT MONTH FROM
Love Inspired

HER UNLIKELY AMISH PROTECTOR
by Jocelyn McClay

Amish nanny Miriam Schrock isn't pleased when handsome bad boy Aaron Raber starts working for the same family as she does. But soon Miriam sees the good man he's become. When his troubled past threatens them both, Aaron must step in to protect the only one who truly believes in him...

THE MYSTERIOUS AMISH NANNY
by Patrice Lewis

Lonely Amish widower Adam Chupp needs help raising his young son. When outsider Ruth Wengerd's car breaks down, she agrees to care for Lucas until it can be repaired. Ruth fits into Amish life easily but is secretive about her past. Will Adam learn the truth about her before he loses his heart?

RESTORING THEIR FAMILY
True North Springs • by Allie Pleiter

Widow Kate Hoyle arrives at Camp True North Springs to heal her grieving family, not the problems of camp chef Seb Costa. But the connection the bold-hearted chef makes with her son—and with her own heart—creates a recipe for love and hope neither one of them expects.

THE BABY PROPOSAL
by Gabrielle Meyer

After his brother's death, Drew Keelan finds himself guardian of his infant nephew. But to keep custody, Drew must get married fast! He proposes a marriage in name only to the baby's aunt, Whitney Emmerson. But when things get complicated, will love help keep their marriage going?

RECLAIMING THE RANCHER'S HEART
by Lisa Carter

Rancher Jack Dolan is surprised when his ex-wife, Kate, returns to town and tells him that they are still married. He suggests that they honor the memory of their late daughter one last time, then go their separate ways. This could be the path to healing—and finding their way back to each other...

THE LONER'S SECRET PAST
by Lorraine Beatty

Eager for a fresh start, single mom Sara Holden comes to Mississippi to help redo her sister's antique shop. And she needs local contractor Luke McBride's help. But the gruff, unfriendly man wants nothing to do with Sara. Can she convince him to come out of seclusion and back to life?

LOOK FOR THESE AND OTHER LOVE INSPIRED BOOKS WHEREVER BOOKS ARE SOLD, INCLUDING MOST BOOKSTORES, SUPERMARKETS, DISCOUNT STORES AND DRUGSTORES.

LICNM1122